TIME'S UP

A MATHILDA HOLIDAY NOVEL

ANNA MCCLUSKEY

---

1.   http://www.annamccluskey.com

2.   http://www.bookbub.com/profile/anna-mccluskey

3.   http://www.facebook.com/annamccluskeyauthor

4.   http://www.sleepyfoxstudios.net

Also by Anna McCluskey

Rhymes With Witch

A Curse, A Key, & A Corkscrew
Witches & Weed
Magic, Mayhem, & A Martini

Mathilda Holiday

Magic Today
The Viper's Head
Hello, Darkness
Brick by Brick
Time's Up

Warrior Mage Librarians

Coming to Kickstarter June 2023
Blood Falls
Gateway to Hell
Snake Island
Devil's Triangle

1.

Mattie swung her sword with her left arm, acutely aware of her dominant right arm, injured and immobilized against her side by a sling. Her opponent dodged it easily and countered with a stroke of her own sword that had Mattie scrambling backward, cursing under her breath.

Sister Regina smirked at her as she swept her sword at Mattie's legs, knocking her to her knees. "Surrender?"

"Not quite," said Mattie. She gritted her teeth, jumped to her feet and spun around, focusing on aiming the wooden practice sword with the same deadly accuracy she usually had with the use of both arms.

This time, she managed to hit the warrior nun on the elbow, causing her to drop her sword.

Sister Regina dived for it and rolled back to her feet, smoothly bringing her weapon around, swinging it toward Mattie's neck.

Mattie brought up her own sword just in time to block it and felt the impact jar all the way up to her shoulder.

Ignoring the discomfort, she attacked with a flurry of thrusts and slashes that had Sister Regina dancing back and forth to parry and block.

Finally feeling like she was getting the hang of the one-handed fighting, Mattie pushed herself and kept at it until she managed to corner Sister Regina in a corner.

With a twist of the wooden sword, she disarmed the nun once again, this time kicking her opponent's sword away and leveling her own at Sister Regina's heart. "Surrender?" she said with a mocking smile.

Sister Regina lifted her hands and smiled back. "Fair enough. If I'd had my mage sight on, of course...."

"Sure," said Mattie, lowering her sword. "But we have to be prepared for anything before heading to the Auditor's bunker, right?

Lansdowne said that Harper spies have had issues using magery in that place in the past."

Sister Regina's lips twisted. "I'd love to know how they manage to tamp down the abilities of spies they don't even know are there, but still maintain their own mage abilities."

The door to the practice room opened and Sister Catherine poked her head in. "Are you two finished? Sister Abigail would like a word with Mattie, and Sister Regina, we have that meeting with the Cardinal."

"I'll head up there in a minute," said Mattie. She grabbed a towel from the stack of clean ones that always sat on the bench against the wall of the studio, wiped her face on it, and then tossed it into the laundry hamper by the door. "Thanks for sparring," she called over her shoulder to Sister Regina as she ambled out.

Sister Regina was peering into the mirror, trying in vain to adjust the ecclesiastical head-dress she wore, which was perpetually crooked. "Anytime," she said absently as she unclipped one of the barrettes that held it in place.

Mattie strode toward the infirmary, hoping the news was that it was time for her sling to come off and she could join her friends and her sister on the front lines at Broken Bunker, the world headquarters of the Auditors.

Well, that is, her sister and her friend Trevor were probably being held at Broken Bunker. And a handful of her other friends were scoping out the place, working on finding a way in so they could mount a rescue.

Mattie had been injured in the initial fight to get them free, when they'd waylaid the train Tillie and Trevor were on. Taking her out of the game had given the kidnappers the distraction they needed to escape.

Now, pushing open the door to the infirmary, Mattie's attention was caught by another occupant of the large room.

"Hi, Madeleine," she said, warily. "Is Sister Abigail around?"

Madeleine nodded back. "She just left, but she'll be back in a minute."

Mattie hesitated, still unsure how to behave around someone who had been the enemy until just a few days ago, when, under a combined truth serum and spell, she had confessed that she wasn't quite as loyal to the Auditor organization as she'd seemed.

Sister Catherine had reacted by treating her as an ally, and she seemed to be responding well to it, but Mattie wasn't so sure. You didn't just go from dedicating your entire life to a cause to suddenly fighting against it just because some nuns were nice to you.

"I don't really like that, you know," said Madeleine abruptly. She was seated on a hospital bed, on top of the blankets, her knees drawn up to her chin, arms wrapped around herself. Her hands formed claws, her fingertips digging into the denim that covered her shins. The former spy looked oddly unlike herself without her leather armor. Almost helpless, like a turtle without its shell.

Mattie blinked. "Don't like what?"

"'Madeleine,'" she said. She shivered, despite the warm room.. "I remember the truth serum stuff. I know you all think that's my name. But do you remember the sequence of it?"

Mattie studied the young woman, watching as she seemed to be making herself as small as she could. Madeleine squirmed under her scrutiny, but Mattie couldn't be sure if she was genuinely tense or if it was all another game. "I wasn't there for your truth seruming, actually," she responded, finally . "I heard about it afterward."

"Well, they asked me for my real name." Madeleine inhaled deeply. "And I told it to them. My name is Chameleon. Then they asked me what name I was born with and they decided that must be the name I should go by. Madeleine."

Mattie nodded slowly. "I see what you mean." She took a cautious step closer. "You have to understand that the other former agents of the Auditors we've talked to have begun to reclaim their first names because the organization took them away. So, for them, it's a statement of freedom, of individuality. But your situation is different."

Madeleine – Chameleon – looked away, staring at a fixed point on the wall, and hugged her knees tighter. "Yes. It is."

Mattie winced. If this was an act, it was very convincing. The amount of tension Chameleon held in her body couldn't possibly be comfortable. Then again, she'd pulled off convincing performances before.

Something about this felt different, though, and Mattie's instincts, honed by a decade of teaching volatile and vulnerable teens, screamed at her to comfort Chameleon. "How old are you?"

Chameleon looked startled. "Twenty-two. Why do you ask?"

She was barely an adult. Mattie's sympathy deepened. The woman was only a few years older than the high school kids she taught English to. But while those kids were finding out who they were, she had been told who she had to be.

"Just curious," said Mattie. She cracked a reluctant smile. "Chameleon suits you."

Chameleon's eyes darted toward Mattie. "What's that supposed to mean?"

"Oh." Mattie blinked again. "I mean, isn't it based on your skillset?" She hesitated, and then sat down on the bed next to Chameleon's. "As a spy, you become whoever you're trying to be, right? Agent Shezza, Polly." She swallowed, trying not to think about how Chameleon had slit Polly's throat in order to take her place.

But such was war, right? Chameleon was a brainwashed victim, no different than any of her other former agent friends. If anything, she'd been brainwashed from an early age, so was to be pitied even more.

And Mattie had seen Polly's body – the kill had been clean and fast, which told her that Chameleon had taken no joy in it, no sadistic pleasure in prolonging it.

"Even now, you keep changing who you are, from the bad-ass spy to the broken-down Madeleine–" Mattie realized how that sounded and lifted her hand to forestall any argument. "I'm sorry, I didn't mean it like that. Just that now you have an opportunity to find *yourself*, right? And you've been other people for so long, it's going to take some time to do that. If 'Chameleon' is who you want to be, then be Chameleon."

Chameleon nodded, a tiny smile appearing on her lips, incongruous beside the visibly taut muscles standing out in her neck. "I guess you're right. I have been myself before, though, you know."

"Oh, yeah?" All at once, Mattie made her decision. Maybe she'd change her mind later, but for the moment, she was going to trust Chameleon.

She pivoted and swung her legs up onto the bed, scooting her butt back so she leaned against the wall. "When was that?"

"When I've been around others like me. The other Special agents." Chameleon sighed, her entire body shuddering as a small amount of her tension eased. "We stood apart from–" She stopped, head turning and eyes widening as the door opened.

A small knife appeared in her hand, as though from nowhere.

The doctor in charge of the infirmary bustled in, pushing a rattling cart full of medical supplies. "Ah, Mattie. Glad you made it up here," said Sister Abigail. "Let's take a look at that arm."

Mattie watched closely as Chameleon's knife disappeared again, even though the woman didn't seem to move a single muscle. She couldn't see where the blade had gone.

Abandoning her cart next to a large, locked cabinet, Sister Abigail strode to Mattie's side and gently pulled off the sling. "How does it feel?"

"It feels fine, honestly," said Mattie, turning her attention resolutely away from Chameleon. Of course the woman was reactive; that didn't mean she wasn't trustworthy.

Mattie gingerly stretched the arm out, moving it back and forth to test it out. The arm had been badly burned in the fight against four Auditor agents, and the Warrior Mage Healers at a hospital in Chicago had stitched her skin back from blistered to new, but it had still been very tender. "In fact," she said, "It feels completely normal now."

"Wonderful." Sister Abigail beamed at Mattie. "That's just wonderful. In that case, I am officially going to clear you to return to the action."

Mattie jumped up. "Yes! Awesome!" She thrust her right arm into the air. "Ol' Two-Arms is back, bitches!"

***

Tillie regarded the tray of food in front of her and sighed. She wasn't sure how long she had been held captive in this small room, but this was the seventh meal that had appeared on the table in front of her since she'd arrived.

That was the only way she could think to track the time, and she'd been carefully counting. It felt like a long time between meals, and that time seemed skewed. Additionally, there had been no breakfast foods, so she was pretty sure they were only feeding her lunch and dinner.

And every other meal had been served with wine, which also argued for lunch and dinner.

So, if she was correctly analyzing the situation, which was a big *if* when dealing with a sketchy secret society that kidnapped people for doing exactly the same things they did, that meant that she was on her fourth day here, and had arrived in the afternoon on Day 1.

Tillie was pretty sure none of the food she'd been given here was drugged, and she was just as sure that the last tray of food they'd given her on the train had been – she had no memory of moving from the train car to the cell she was in now.

All she knew was that at some point, the train had stopped and she'd been divested of her regular clothing – and all of the useful things she'd had in her hidden pockets, including the beacon spell that she'd hoped had been leading her sister and friends to her location – and dressed in this horrible pink-and-beige striped jumpsuit.

Tillie had to admit, as she looked around the cell, that this wasn't the worst kidnapping situation she'd ever found herself in. At least this room was relatively comfortable – who was she kidding; it was luxuriously appointed – and had an attached bathroom, complete with a clawfoot tub and a separate shower stall with a rainfall shower.

In fact, it was suspiciously comfortable. It didn't mesh with what she knew about the Auditor organization at all.

As Tillie picked up her fork and began to eat the lasagna – which was very good – she tallied up in her head everything she knew.

She was in the custody of the Auditors.

Even though she hadn't seen any actual people, it was obvious that this was the work of the society of mages against which she'd been fighting for the past couple of months, ever since the first time they'd tried – and failed – to kidnap her. Even if there'd been no other evidence of that, the hideous jumpsuit was clearly designed by those tacky courtiers.

The Auditors *claimed* to exist in order to maintain balance in the mage world. They alleged that their mission was to prevent mages from practicing multiple disciplines, which they preached could destroy the world.

But as Tillie learned more about the organization, she had discovered that those in their upper echelons practiced all three mage powers with no qualms at all. The organization existed to maintain its own power and nothing else.

She had run afoul of them when she, a natural seer, had dared to begin to study how to use spells and stitches. They had assigned a team of agents to kidnap her, to bring her in for re-education and turn her into another agent like themselves.

Instead, a rogue agent, Giovani, had warned her and she had escaped her fate, running from the team and evading them all across the country. Unfortunately, she had managed to drag both her best friend and her twin sister into the fight as well, and she felt simultaneously guilty about bringing them in now and about keeping this side of her life from them for the past fifteen years.

Tillie gave her head an abrupt shake; she was woolgathering, like a stitcher.

She was a seer, and seers typically lived in the future, planning out every detail of their lives, always being prepared for any eventuality. That matched their abilities to see the near future when they wanted to, or to see spells and scry out far-away events in the present.

Stitchers, like her best friend, Trevor, lived in the past, remembering details of what had been, and their power lay in using hand gestures to affect the fabric of time and space. She knew she was becoming more like that because she'd been using the other two mage disciplines.

The other discipline, spelling, involved using words, spoken or thought, in order to affect the world around them. Spellers, like her sister, Mattie, tended to live in the moment.

But Mattie, though new to magery, was taking to it quickly and naturally, and what's more, she was learning all three disciplines together and becoming less speller-like by the day.

Tillie took another bite of pasta, savoring the complex flavors of the rich, meaty tomato sauce and creamy ricotta cheese.

This place, whatever it was, must have one hell of a chef.

She finished the lasagna and its accompanying roasted cauliflower, and wiped her lips carefully on the linen napkin on the tray.

Then she moved on to the small, elegant slice of flourless chocolate cake, alternating bites with sips of red wine. A pinot noir, if she wasn't mistaken, and a very good one.

***

Trevor hoped that Tillie was getting the same food he was. That lasagna was phenomenal and the rich chocolate dessert even better. The wine served alongside it was perfection as well.

He knew he shouldn't be drinking; he needed to stay alert. But one glass of wine was hardly going to impair him, and frankly this was the first time he'd ever been kidnapped and his nerves were absolutely shot.

He supposed Tillie wasn't as rattled as he was – she'd been kidnapped a couple of times in her life as an escort, and that didn't even count the first time the Auditors had *tried* to kidnap her, when he and Mattie had gone after her and discovered this whole damn world of magery and secret societies.

Trevor still couldn't quite believe that his best friend had kept this from him for so many years. But he couldn't blame her.

He understood that she'd discovered magery at a time in her life when she'd been particularly vulnerable. They'd been in their early twenties, and she'd just gotten out of an abusive relationship and was picking up the pieces of her life.

He had been so busy with grad school and everything, and he knew he hadn't been there for her the way she'd needed. He resolutely pushed the guilt away and sipped his wine.

Remembering the pain that had buried Tillie in those days, when they'd lived together in that tiny apartment in faraway St. Louis, Trevor closed his eyes. He'd done his best to comfort Tillie, but he knew he'd been exactly the wrong blend of overprotective-but-distracted.

No wonder she hadn't confided in him.

But surely opportunities had come up in the years in between, the years in which they'd remained best friends, seeing each other every single day, even as they'd gotten their own living spaces, him buying a small house in south city, and her moving into a condo in the trendy downtown loft district.

Tillie had included him in every other aspect of her life – *that he knew about, anyway,* said a small voice in his head, which he shoved back. She'd told him when she'd decided that she could make more money as an escort than as a massage therapist.

Surely that was just as illicit as magery.

Trevor shook his head and stood up, abruptly. This train of thought was pointless. What he needed to be doing was working on a plan to get out of this cell, comfortable as it was, and find Tillie.

He had already tried tapping out their secret codes on the walls, as soon as he'd woken up to find himself in this small room, dressed in the beige-and-pink coveralls of a prisoner. He supposed he should be glad they weren't orange, anyway.

Trevor's lips twisted wryly as he pictured Tillie's distaste at the outfit she'd probably also been dressed in.

Just in case, he moved toward the nearest wall of his cell and tapped out the morse code again. *Do you know me? Pineapple, turquoise, scissors.*

He waited, but there was no response, as there had been on the train here, when they'd been put into adjacent rooms.

He moved on to the next wall, and the next. Then he grabbed his wine and sat down on the narrow bed with a sigh.

Nothing to do but wait.

***

Sister Margaret paced impatiently around the motel room. She found it difficult to sit still at the best of times, and this was not that.

This also wasn't how she'd pictured her very first time leaving her home town of St. Louis – on a dead-end trip to rescue two people from a hidden bunker.

Okay, the secret-society-hidden-bunker thing was pretty cool, and she really did care about Tillie and Trevor, but she'd always imagined herself on a clandestine mission for the Vatican, maybe as a newly minted Warrior Mage Librarian or something equally interesting and prestigious.

And she assumed she'd be with an elite team of other Warrior Mages in a carefully planned out quest for some kind of incredibly important document or magical artifact or....

Well, not sitting in a motel room with three very-competent-but-not-really-elite mages with no fancy titles, painstakingly scrying out every square mile of surrounding countryside trying to figure out where, specifically, the bunker actually was.

Amy had been there before, but she'd been stitched in and out by a court member whose only job was to stitch people in and out.

She'd been driven to the stitch-site with a blindfold on, so she only had a general idea of where the bunker was.

Giovani looked up from where he sat at the table in the middle of the room, bent over a scrying stone. "Are you okay?" he asked, eyebrows raised.

"Yeah, I'm fine," she sighed. "I'm just bored. I can take over for you there, if you want to stretch your legs and grab a bite to eat."

"That'd be great." Giovani stood and extended his arms and torso toward the ceiling.

Amy shut her book and stood up as well. "I could use a snack too," she said. "Nicole?"

Nicole's head snapped up from her own book. "What?"

"Must be something interesting," said Sister Margaret, striding toward her. "What have you got there?"

Nicole closed the book, holding her spot with a finger, and held it up so Sister Margaret could see the cover. "It is, actually. A textbook for children of the court, talking about using all three mage disciplines together."

"Those fucking hypocrites." Sister Margaret eyed the gray cover of the old-fashioned hardcover book, which read *A Beginning Morpher's Primer.*

Nicole shrugged. "We knew that, right? At least we're learning from them. This is talking right now about how you can use a scrying stone, a spell, and a stitch to teleport farther than your average stitcher can."

"That's handy," said Giovani. "But only if you carry a scrying stone around with you."

"They're a little bit cumbersome," Sister Margaret observed. "But then again, if you can stitch, you don't need to carry it in your pocket. Just have it somewhere within range and stitch it to you."

She was a little surprised Giovani hadn't thought of that. Of all of the Foxes, as the group of former Auditor agents was starting to be called, he was the one who seemed to take to morphing the easiest. He almost seemed like a natural morpher, if such a thing could be possible, rather than the natural stitcher that he considered himself.

Sister Margaret sat down at the table and turned on her seer sight, moving the scrying stone a little bit, positioning it to her own preferred angle as the others filed out of the room in search of food.

"Let's find this fucking bunker," she murmured.

2.

Mattie tracked down Sister Catherine, who was in the gym directing a group of Harpers – another secret society made up of former Auditor agents, who had recently made contact and presented themselves as allies – as they packed up various bladed weaponry into a back and yellow plastic tote box.

"I'm here!" she said, cheerfully. "Cleared for action and ready for duty. When do we ship out?"

Sister Catherine smiled. "Glad to hear it. Not for another week, probably. We don't want to go in half-cocked. Best to take our time and do it right."

Mattie frowned. "What about Tillie and Trevor? They're in there, being subjected to who knows what kind of torture and brainwashing bullshit! We have to get them out!"

"I disagree," interjected Father Sean, another warrior mage who had been with them since they'd taken out the court at their St. Louis headquarters. He sat on a tall stool behind a nearby table with some kind of complicated apparatus on it, apparently for sharpening axe blades. He didn't look up from the blade he was engaged in sharpening as he continued. "Amy and Madeleine–"

"Chameleon," Mattie interrupted. "She wants to be called Chameleon."

Father Sean blinked several times, studying Mattie, even as his hands continued running the blade over the stones. "She does? Why would anyone want to be called that?"

"It's her name," said Mattie.

"Her code name, I thought," said Sister Catherine.

Mattie shrugged. "All I know is that she asked to be called that and that she thinks of it as her real name. It's none of my business why someone wants to be known by any certain name, but it's no skin off my nose to do so."

"All right," said Father Sean. "Both Amy and Chameleon stated separately that Broken Bunker wasn't a re-education facility. It's the only station in the country that either of them knew about where no one is taken to be brainwashed and trained up to be an agent."

"Okay, so they're not being trained," said Mattie. "That doesn't mean they're not being tortured or starved or something. Or scheduled to be executed."

Now Father Sean did pause. "Do they do that?"

Mattie threw up her hands. "How the fuck should I know?"

"It is a possibility we should probably consider," Sister Catherine pointed out. "And maybe ask Chameleon."

"You don't think Chameleon would have mentioned it when we asked for information before?" asked one of the Harpers, a woman with pale skin, slicked back dark hair, and the same black suit that all of the members of that particular group of former Auditor agents seemed to favor.

Sister Catherine sighed. "It's a tricky balance, turning an enemy into an ally. It's not like you can just flip a switch, and suddenly they're friendly and telling you everything they know and you can immediately trust them implicitly. Every instinct you have tells you that you shouldn't trust anything they say, and then somehow you feel betrayed if they don't tell you everything you want to know, but you have to remember that you were their enemy at the same time they were yours."

"And then there's the whole 'Do you set a guard on them?' dilemma," Father Sean added. "On the one hand, it could be bad not to if they're not as much on your side as you thought, but on the other, if they feel like you don't trust them, they're less likely to cooperate fully."

"And it's even trickier when you know that they're used to being deceitful," said Sister Catherine. "Chameleon was a spy, and a damn good one. The only way to know for sure that she's truly on our side now would be to keep her under truth serum all day, every day, and that's neither kind nor practical. We just have to stick to kindness and hope it's as effective as we'd like."

Mattie drummed her fingers on the table beside her, fixing her eyes on a stack of freeze-dried meals in shiny mylar packaging, and tried to force some patience into her mind.

This was all well and good, but her entire being was screaming that action needed to be taken and it needed to happen NOW.

Father Sean abruptly seemed to notice her impatience. "The soonest we could leave would be a week, dear," he said. "I know that's not what you want to hear, but the fact is that prepping for war takes time. We need to get the supplies packed into the vans, supplies for an entire army, and for a long time; we have no idea how long we'll be out there at the bunker. Don't worry, though – once we do get moving, we'll move fast."

"This isn't our first rodeo," added Sister Catherine. "Father Sean will be leading this campaign and he's done this, oh, five or six times before, haven't you?"

He nodded. "Six, actually. I'm sorry, Mattie, but this is how we need to do this."

Mattie nodded. She didn't like it, but he was probably right. "Well, boss, just tell me how I can help."

***

Trevor drained the last of his wine and then stood to replace it on the tray that still sat in the center of the small round table.

As he stood up, however, the tray disappeared, stitched back to, he assumed, some kind of central kitchen.

The empty glass remained in his hand and he studied it. There was something here.

A tiny germ of an idea was beginning to form in his head, but he couldn't quite grasp it yet.

Trevor sat down, turning the glass around in his fingers, admiring the graceful curve of the stem and bulb, waiting for his mind to catch up with itself.

Then he jumped to his feet again, dropping the glass in his excitement. It shattered on the concrete floor of the cell.

Of course! Trevor usually put the glass back on the tray when he was done. Then the tray *and everything touching it* would be stitched out to be cleaned up and used again for the next meal.

All he needed to do was hold on tight to the tray next time around, and he'd be out of this cell.

The next meal wouldn't be for hours.

He should get some sleep.

Stepping carefully over the broken glass, Trevor made his way into the bathroom to shower and get ready for bed.

If everything went well, tomorrow would be a big day.

***

Sister Margaret jumped up from her chair. "There! There it fucking is!"

She spun around in the middle of the motel room, her arms flung outward, and smacked her pinky finger on the dresser. She stopped spinning and frowned at the dresser, shaking out her hand. "Ouch. Fucking piece of plywood. Fuck."

She studied the injured finger, but the pain was already starting to abate. Wasn't that how it always was with fingers and toes? Hurt like a motherfucker for just a few seconds and then you're fine.

"Are you okay?" asked Nicole. She got up from her chair, tucked away in the corner of the room, where she'd been reading. "What did you find?"

Sister Margaret whirled toward her, grinning and moving her eyes momentarily out of seer mode. She'd forgotten the other woman was in the room and had been so focused on her task that she hadn't even noticed her in her sight. "Check this shit out. It's a fucking door in the hillside, like a damn hobbit house. Just right fucking here in Utah. Nasty hobbitses."

"Really?" Nicole followed her back to the table.

Sister Margaret turned her seer sight back on and peered into the stone once more, willing it to show her the door she'd just seen. She felt Nicole's hand as she touched her shoulder, and she "tossed" the image toward her.

Nicole projected it onto the wall, and Sister Margaret looked up at the expanded landscape. "There. Do you see it? The bastards painted it the same dusty brown as the rest of this desolate wasteland, so it blends the fuck in, but it's there, right? Clear as day."

"I see it!" Nicole moved her hand down Sister Margaret's arm, keeping contact as she moved closer to the wall to examine the picture.

Sister Margaret was a little startled at the intimacy of the touch, which felt almost caress-like, but she shrugged it off. She was pretty sure Nicole didn't swing that way, and people hardly ever hit on her anymore, once they realized she was a nun.

And it was weird how many people were shocked to find a nun who was gay. That didn't go away just because you took an oath not to act on it.

If it had been Tillie touching her like that, she'd be out of the room and halfway down the street by now. No way was she going to stick around and have her arm stroked by a gorgeous former escort who clearly wanted her – she was celebate, but still human, and while temptation didn't hit often, that one was . . . well. Best nip that line of thinking in the bud.

"I'm going to zoom out," she said aloud. "Get a good bead on what's around it, so we know exactly where it is."

"Good plan," said Nicole. She moved her hand back a few inches so it rested on Sister Margaret's wrist bracer, and sat down beside her at the table. "See if you can get it all the way out so we can see the town and which direction it lies from here."

Sister Margaret blinked several times in a row, zooming out slowly, in stages, so that they would be able to keep tabs on where the small door was.

"There!" said Nicole, pointing with her free hand. "You can see the road looks like it's about two hundred feet off, and it's just about, oh, two miles west of here."

"And that's the highway, there," agreed Sister Margaret. "So, that's good; it's not actually that far off the main drag."

The door opened and Giovani and Amy entered, each carrying a greasy paper bag. The aroma of fast food french fries filled the room.

"Did you find something?" asked Amy, eagerly tossing her bag on one of the beds and hurrying forward to study the projected image.

"Right there," said Nicole, pointing to the spot where Sister Margaret knew the door was. Zoomed out as it was, you really couldn't see anything beyond a little darker brown dot that looked more like a dried-out shrub than anything else.

Sister Margaret zoomed back in until the door was visible again.

Giovani and Amy inhaled sharply in unison.

"I'll be damned," said Giovani, softly. "Who would have thought it would be that open? I was expecting something more like a slice in the sod that would turn out to be a magical garage door."

"Okay, now we know where it is physically," said Sister Margaret. "The next step is to scry out the inside, find a spot Amy recognizes, and stitch our asses in there."

"Actually, I think the next step is dinner," said Nicole. She removed her hand from Sister Margaret's wrist and the image on the wall faded.

Amy picked up the bag of food, and Giovani set his down on the table, opening it up and passing out burgers and fries.

As Sister Margaret pulled her bacon cheeseburger from its crinkly foil wrapper, her mind raced into the future, thinking through all the possible ways this mission could go belly-up.

3.

Tillie awoke, opened her eyes, and assessed her bodily state. No headache or dry mouth, so there hadn't been any drugs in last night's meal. She stretched. No stiffness in her joints or muscles, so the small amount of exercise she'd been able to get in such small quarters was keeping her limber.

She threw off the comforter and sheets, which had a thread count as high as the ones in her own home, and stepped onto the concrete floor.

This imprisonment was such a bizarre blend of luxury and austerity. The floors were cement, like an unfinished basement, but the furnishings were comfortable to the point of opulence.

She'd only been given one garment to wear, and it was hideous but made of soft cotton. No undergarments or footwear had been made available.

The jumpsuit was getting smelly after so many days of wear, even though Tillie had begun doing her work-outs naked so as to not sweat in it.

She'd considered sleeping naked as well, but was afraid she'd be stitched out into a new place during the night and while she was comfortable in her skin, clothing did provide a certain protection against the elements, and it was best not to be without it.

Tillie stripped and began her krav maga routine, following it up with some soothing yoga, and ending with stillness in a lotus position, remaining in meditation for some time.

Finally, she stood, stretched, and ambled into the bathroom to shower.

She snagged the jumpsuit from the back of the chair along the way. She had soap and water. Might as well wash it; who knew how long she was going to be in this place?

Besides, the time in this cell with little to do was starting to scrape away at her psyche. She needed occupation. Laundry was better than staring at the wall.

***

Trevor paced his small-but-oddly-luxurious cell. This whole thing didn't mesh at all with how the others had described their time of being processed and re-educated by the Auditor organization.

Amy had told him that she'd been put in a bare padded cell, much like the one Tillie had been put into in St. Louis the first time she'd been taken. Of course, Tillie had been taken by the Foxes, not the actual Auditors, and she'd been set free soon after, as she and Nicole had hatched their plot to work together.

Amy had been kept in the padded cell and essentially tortured – they'd used sleep deprivation, odd light patterns, erratic and disrupted meal times, loud noises, and all kinds of other methods of keeping her confused and off-balance.

Giovani and others had mentioned similar experiences, so it was clear that the organization had a routine, and that this wasn't it.

Hopefully that meant he also wasn't going to be subjected to any other brainwashing techniques either.

He had cleaned up the shards of glass, tucking a couple of the larger pieces into the large belly pocket of his jumpsuit in case he needed a weapon, but he avoided the spot the wine glass had broken anyway.

Couldn't be too careful, given his barefoot state.

Trevor went over his plan again in his head as he paced. He wouldn't be able to enact it until after lunch, since they never gave him breakfast.

Fortunately, he'd always had a pretty reliable internal clock – he now knew that was part of being a stitcher – and even without windows, he was sure it would be only a couple more hours.

Then he'd be, if not free, at least out of this tiny room.

***

Mattie's fingers ached and her face dripped sweat in the oppressive humidity as she unloaded another dolly of the sharp-edged plastic crates into another of the convent's plain white vans. She had no idea where the nuns kept these vans usually, but they just kept showing up and then driving off once they were loaded up with supplies.

This van was being filled with medical supplies. The last one had been case after case of bottled water.

Much as she hated to wait, Mattie had to admit that these nuns knew what they were doing.

She turned to grab the next box from the stack, and was startled to see Chameleon standing behind her.

"Hi," said Chameleon. She bit her lip and then sighed. "I want to help, but I'm not sure how."

Mattie shrugged. "I'm helping by putting these crates on the van."

Chameleon frowned. "You're using muscle and not magery?"

"I'm not a stitcher," said Mattie. "I mean, I can stitch, but this is a lot to–"

"You're a speller, right?" said Chameleon. Without waiting for an answer, her hands began to glow and the entire stack of boxes levitated, moving swiftly around Mattie and into the van, sliding to a halt on the van floor.

The glow around Chameleon's hands pulsed and the crates began to rearrange themselves into a sturdy formation.

Mattie blinked. The entire process had taken about seven seconds. She'd been lugging crates around for a couple of hours.

Sister Regina wheeled another dolly of boxes out of the gym, and stopped abruptly. "What happened to the ones that were out here?" she demanded.

"They're loaded up," said Mattie. "Chameleon floated them in."

Pursing her lips, Sister Regina studied the younger woman. "You floated them in?"

Chameleon nodded, her shoulders hunching slightly, eyes darting around as though looking for a reason the nun was so upset about it.

Mattie wasn't sure why she seemed so angry either.

"Out here?" Sister Regina crossed her arms. "Out in the parking lot of our convent, right here, where everyone in the surrounding houses can see us? With all these cars driving past? You floated a bunch of boxes off the ground and into a van?"

Oh. Right. That's why they hadn't been doing that.

Chameleon's eyes narrowed and she pulled her shoulders back, drew herself up to her full height, and opened her mouth.

Mattie stepped forward hastily, putting a restraining hand on Chameleon's arm. Sister Regina tended to have the same effect on her, honestly; the woman was more irritating than a screaming child on an airplane. But that was just who she was, and if Chameleon was going to stick around, she'd have to interact with Sister Regina a lot.

"She's not used to being out in the open," Mattie interceded before Chameleon could say anything she might regret later. "She grew up in a magical secret society. Cut her some slack."

Sister Regina rolled her eyes and muttered something under her breath.

"What was that?" asked Mattie, sharply.

"She better get used to it fast," snapped Sister Regina. "Sister Margaret isn't here, and Sister Helen isn't going to put up with these kinds of slip-ups."

"Do not worry about me," said Chameleon. "I will not endanger your operation."

Mattie frowned. Was Chameleon suddenly sporting a German accent? She shrugged it off.

"See?" said Mattie. "She's sorry, and it won't happen again."

Grumbling, Sister Regina took the empty dolly from Mattie and rolled it out, leaving the two of them to empty off the new one – by hand, this time.

"I didn't say I was sorry," said Chameleon. "And I am used to working out in the open, you know. As a Special agent, I am almost always out in the field."

"Makes sense," said Mattie, reaching for a crate. It was definitely some kind of accent. "You're welcome, by the way."

Chameleon's lips curved in a small smile. "*Danke*, Mattie. You know, you can still levitate the boxes, but just do them one at a time, and keep a hand on them so it looks like you're carrying them. It will be easier on your hands and arms. And you'll sweat less."

"My hands will still glow," Mattie pointed out. "Why are you suddenly German, by the way?"

Chameleon froze for a moment and then shivered, hugging herself briefly before dropping her arms and turning away so Mattie saw only her profile. "It's a sunny day," she said, still using the clipped German accent. "Probably no one out there will notice the glow, and even if they do, people are great at explaining impossible things to themselves. I bet you saw magery lots of times before you knew what you were seeing, and you never even knew it."

"Huh." As Mattie thought that over, she crouched down and spelled the box, floating it a teensy bit above her fingers as she mimed picking it up and putting it in the back of the van. Then she used another spell to scoot it over to the opposite side, shielding the open door with her body to hide it from prying eyes of mundane passersby.

Chameleon hadn't addressed the accent, but she wasn't going to push it. The woman was clearly uncomfortable. Maybe putting on a character helped.

"I've seen movies," said Chameleon, abruptly.

Mattie blinked at her. "Oh," she said. She stepped back to make room for Chameleon to load up the two crates she'd just levitated. "Okay."

"Most of the field work I've done has been among agents or Specials," said Chameleon as she maneuvered the boxes into the van. "I haven't been around outsiders very much. But I've seen movies. And TV. I've studied how the outside world works, and it's not so different from the way the organization functions, but on a larger scale. Both worlds are broken."

"Broken?" Mattie pondered that as she switched spots with Chameleon, lifting up two crates herself with her magery this time as well. "You may be right."

"It's the same," said Chameleon. "The people in power keep the power. The people underneath are, for the most part, completely fine with that because they see a small minority of their own rising up, as small segments of the aristocracy fall, sacrificed by the highest elite, the untouchable, in order to maintain that illusion."

"That," said Mattie, slowly, "is very astute." She paused to push some stray bits of hair away from her face.

"Special agents like myself come from the high court, you know," said Chameleon. "All of us are the offspring of courtiers, selected from among the high court children for our intelligence, plucked from a life of luxury and indolence to work among the lowest caste of the organization: the agents."

Something about what Chameleon was saying sounded rehearsed, like it was a speech she'd made before, maybe aloud, but definitely internally, many times before. Mattie also couldn't help but notice that, while she was still speaking with an accent, it was fainter than it had been.

"And we're grateful for it," Chameleon continued. "Have you seen how the high court lives? They have nothing to do but give in to their vices. Between intrigue, machinations, and recreational dueling, the only way you can make it past your teens is by stepping on the necks of the others or by being a completely useless idiot who isn't worth stepping on."

"When you say 'high court,'" said Mattie. "As opposed to . . . ?"

"Working court," said Chameleon, stepping forward with two more crates. "The organization has three tiers. Agents are the new recruits; the ones who are brought in from the outside world. Agents make up the bulk of the organization, and some are assigned to help recruit more, while others stay in the stations, ensuring that the organization runs like the well-oiled machine it is. The working court supervises those agents. They find mages out in the world who are likely morphing and can therefore be taken in and trained as new agents, and assign field agents to take them. They oversee the training once the new recruits are brought in. And they serve as guards and servants for the high court. The working court comes from the agents and they serve as a buffer between the agents and the high court. Their children and the children of the few high courtiers who manage to make it to adulthood are the high court."

Mattie turned to grab another pair of boxes, but they had emptied the dolly in record time. She propped herself against its handles. "And you're a Special agent."

Chameleon nodded. "Special agents are aptly named. We are few, but we are a completely different beast." She paused. "No pun intended."

Mattie laughed. "I'm really starting to like you, Chameleon. Just goes to show – life is full of surprises, isn't it?"

Chameleon thought about this for a moment. "Yes, I suppose it is. Shall we go and grab more of these containers?"

***

Sister Margaret stared into the scrying stone, moving down the hallways of Broken Bunker, Nicole's hand on her shoulder, projecting the images she saw onto the wall for the rest of the group.

The completely useless images. She couldn't see into any rooms. Why couldn't she see into *any* rooms? And why not a blanket spell over the entire bunker?

She could see no reason why they would have sight shields that didn't extend to the hallways, unless it was embedded into a larger spell that for some reason they didn't want extending to the hallways.

And of course, they didn't have this spell on the bunker all the time. Tillie and Amy had been able to scry into the library just a few days ago, from a longer range.

Something had happened to put their guard up, prompting them to lock down on scrying.

Had they noticed the books missing? Or was it something else?

Whatever it was, it was going to make it harder to rescue Tillie and Trevor, and harder to surprise the court when their army of Warrior Mages, Harpers, Foxes, and assorted other volunteers arrived next week to lay siege to the place.

4.

Trevor inhaled sharply as his lunch tray arrived on the table in front of him. If the standard pattern continued, he would be given about an hour to eat, and then he could make his escape.

He knew he should eat.

He wasn't sure he could.

And he couldn't count on past patterns being followed. Best to put everything in place first.

Trevor carefully removed the dishes from the tray – a napkin-rolled set of silverware, a large plate containing a pork chop smothered in a deliciously thyme-scented creamy mushroom sauce, a smaller plate holding a colorful salad, and a blue bottle of mineral water.

Then he sat down at the table, slipping the tray onto his lap and holding tightly to it with his left hand. Still holding on, he used his right hand to unroll the napkin, the silverware clattering together as it fell onto the wooden table.

Then he picked up the fork. Might as well at least try to eat. Who knew when he'd have another chance.

***

Tillie sat naked at her table, the freshly cleaned jumpsuit hanging to dry in the bathroom. She eyed her pork chop with distaste. The sauce smelled amazing, but pork was not her favorite protein, and it had never really agreed with her stomach.

Her stomach was churning enough already, and she was trying to ignore the acidic panic she could feel rising from her belly, growing and growing by the minute.

Quashing down the anxiety, she started on her salad instead, putting all of her focus on savoring the beautiful, peppery nasturtium flowers the chef had scattered among the greens, tomatoes, cucumbers, and briny kalamata olives.

Then she scraped the mushrooms off the pork and ate them on their own.

Finally, she finished off the mineral water, stood up, and began her krav maga exercises once again, giving herself not an instant to give into the mounting hysteria that she knew was coming.

No, she told herself. It wouldn't come. She'd get out of here first.

Somehow, someone would get her out. Or she'd figure out a way to get herself out.

And in the meantime, she'd just keep moving.

***

Mattie and Chameleon finished loading all the boxes that were ready into the vans in record time and adjourned to a corner of the gym, where a break area had been set up for the workers with a couple of beanbag chairs and a snack table.

Sammy, a newbie mage who had begun taking spelling lessons from the nuns and must have been helping organize boxes, was already seated there, munching on a granola bar and scrolling through something on his phone.

Mattie pulled out her own phone. "I should text Sister Margaret for an update on their mission."

"They were planning to scry out the bunker today?" asked Chameleon. She had settled into a slightly deeper version of her regular voice with a very slight German inflection, like someone who had been born overseas but had lived locally for decades.

"Yes," said Mattie without looking up from her text. "I know you already told Sister Catherine that you don't know the exact geographic location, but do you know anything about the layout of it?"

She finished her text and sent it.

"Some," said Chameleon. "I grew up there."

Mattie stared at Chameleon. "Well, that seems like information that would have been helpful to have from the start."

Chameleon shook her head. "It changes often. They are constantly renovating Broken Bunker, excavating new areas and abandoning old ones. It is built in an abandoned coal mine, and areas sometimes collapse or become unstable. They use magery combined with new technology to improve it, but it's not a perfect system. There are areas now that are newly dug, which will probably last much longer, and I know they found some natural caves, which will be even more effective, but the original bunker, where I lived as a child? That's basically gone."

Mattie frowned. "How long ago was Amy stationed there? Could it even have changed since then?"

"I don't know," said Chameleon.

Her phone dinged, and Mattie glanced at it. "Sister Margaret says that she can't scry into any rooms, only the hallways."

"Really." Chameleon's eyebrows shot up. "Isn't that interesting? Is there a computer I could use?"

"Uh, probably," said Mattie. She looked around and called out to the closest nun she recognized. "Sister Regina? Is there a computer lab or something around here? Or a communal laptop we could borrow?"

"The computer lab in the school is closed and all the computers will be locked up," said the nun, adjusting her perpetually crooked wimple. "There's a shared computer in the convent library you can use. It's ancient, but it functions."

"Thanks." Mattie braced her hands and feet on the floor and leveraged herself out of the beanbag chair with some difficulty. "This way," she said to Chameleon, jerking her head toward the door.

***

Trevor paced to and fro, back and forth across his cell, carrying his tray, both hands clenched tightly on the sides. His now-empty lunch dishes were stacked neatly on the table.

And then suddenly he was stepping toward a surprised-looking thin-haired white man dressed in a green scrub-like uniform with a black rubber apron over it.

"*Zut-alors*!" shouted the man, skipping backward on the textured black mat that was laid down over the concrete floor. He tripped slightly over the edge of the mat and grabbed the large stainless steel industrial sink next to him, steadying himself. Raising his hands, the man let out a string of rapid French that Trevor couldn't follow.

He was better with reading medieval French than deciphering the modern language anyway.

Before Trevor had time to do or say anything, the dishwasher's hands glowed and a fireball flew straight for his head.

Ducking, Trevor rushed toward the man, smacking him on the top of the head with the tray that he still held, and then skidding to a stop just in time, an instant before he would have crashed into a tall wire shelving unit covered in more dishes and more trays.

He pivoted and saw that the other mage, while looking a little shaken, was still intact and standing. And three more people dressed in a similar fashion had just arrived in the doorway behind him.

"*Zut-alors*, indeed," Trevor muttered. He should have known his luck at finding only one person to fight wouldn't hold.

He tossed the tray into the sink and shifted into a krav maga ready stance. He wasn't as good at the hand-to-hand fighting as Tillie was, but they had attended classes together, and he could hold his own.

Plus, he'd been practicing with Sister Catherine, blending stitching and krav maga together into a unique magical fighting style that was all his, as well as working on swordwork with Sister Margaret.

With a wordless shout, Trevor pivoted, making a stitching gesture with his left hand as he smashed his right into the side of his closest opponent's head. This time, the Frenchman crumpled to the ground.

As he finished his pivot, he saw that his stitch had also been successful, as the woman who had been leading the charge into the dishroom tripped over the mat, which had lifted itself off the ground in front of her.

The other two mages hefted knives, and Trevor cautiously held himself back to see what their move would be.

Hopefully, there was a reason they were working in the kitchen and not out in the field, doing the fighting work of an Auditor agent. Then he thought of the delicious food he'd been eating, and hesitated. Could he really attack such artists?

In his moment of hesitancy, the slender brunette in front of him threw her paring knife straight at his shoulder. It glowed, as did her hands, and even as he ducked, it corrected its course, following him, and struck him just below his right clavicle, burying itself up to the hilt.

Howling in pain, Trevor staggered backward, and the woman advanced upon him, closely followed by the other mage, a pimply teenage boy who must have just begun learning the ropes of cookery.

Trevor's vision began to blur as he regained his footing, and he took another careful step backward. That final step took him back against the drying rack and his groping hand closed around the handle of some kind of kitchen implement.

"Please don't be a whisk," he muttered. He pulled the utensil out and was relieved to see that it was a large carving fork.

Brandishing it in his left hand – and trying not to move his right arm at all – Trevor croaked out, "Stay back!"

"Oh, please," scoffed the chef. She stepped right up to him and grabbed the handle of her knife, twisting it.

"FUCK!" Trevor bellowed. "What is your fucking problem?"

He collapsed backward against the shelf, his body knocking down stacks of dishes, which crashed to the floor.

The chef grinned, obviously the kind of sick fuck who enjoyed torturing people. Trevor felt more betrayed than he ever had before, knowing that the wonderful food he'd been eating came from this monster.

One corner of his brain was vaguely amused by this feeling. The rest was busy with pain.

"You're not supposed to be here," said the boy.

"He knows that," said the chef. She leaned forward, pushing the knife forward and then pulled it abruptly out of Trevor's flesh, watching closely for his reaction.

Trevor gritted his teeth and clamped his mouth shut over the torrent of curses that threatened to explode out of him. He wouldn't give her the pleasure again.

Glaring at her, he focused instead on moving his other hand, the one with the carving fork, surreptitiously backward, as she moved her face close to his.

"Think you're awfully clever, don't you? Getting ol' Agent Brown to stitch you in with the tray? You think you're the first person to ever think of that?"

Trevor inhaled deeply, staring into his assailant's eyes, and then swiftly swung the fork forward, stabbing it into her abdomen.

The woman reeled backward, her eyes wide, hands grasping at her belly.

Trevor knew he hadn't gotten it deep enough to do any real damage; she would recover quickly.

Clenching his jaw against the pain in his shoulder, he moved the fingers of his good hand, stitching one of the shards of wineglass from the pocket of his jumpsuit directly into the woman's left eye.

As she screamed and fell to her knees, Trevor gripped the shelf behind him, using it to pull himself upright, and lurched forward, holding onto his injury and shoving past the kid, who was just standing frozen in place.

Trevor paused to grab a folded towel from a tidy stack on a steel table beside the door and then staggered into the kitchen, searching for a way out and a safe place to bandage up and regroup.

5.

"This is ridiculous," said Sister Margaret. She jumped to her feet, moving her eyes back out of seer mode and rubbing her temples. She pulled the elastic band off the end of her long braid and began to undo it, hoping that loosening her hair would help with the headache that had been steadily growing all day long. "All of these damn hallways look the same. They're all fucking hallways. We're never going to find a specific spot that is distinctive enough for you to stitch us all in."

"Sorry," said Amy. "I need some kind of defining feature to grab onto, and all the rooms I've actually been to seem to be shielded against stitching in now."

"I know," said Sister Margaret. "I just think maybe we need a new plan."

"So, what do you propose?" asked Giovani, leaning back in his chair.

"Why don't we just go in through the door?" said Nicole. "I know that it'll mean giving up the element of stealth, but–"

Nicole pulled the scrying stone toward herself, her own eyes going blank as she gazed into it.

Amy, who sat beside Nicole, put a hand on her shoulder and projected the picture onto the wall, the stitcher's lips moving with the effort of spelling.

Sister Margaret narrowed her eyes as she studied the image of the area just inside the entrance. "There are only three guards. We could take them out easily and then that would buy us some time."

"Exactly," said Nicole. "Let's watch and see their routine. If we can take out the guards just after they change shifts, we'll have an entire shift, however long that may be, until they discover our presence."

"And then, even though they may know we're there, they won't know where," said Sister Margaret. "I like it."

Giovani pointed to a large black circle on the wall behind a guard's head. "That looks like a panic button. We'll have to take that out."

"No problem," said Sister Margaret. "Those are easy to short out with a spell, which is why I don't bother to use them at the convent."

"I'll take out the panic button," Nicole volunteered.

"Once we're inside, we can find a spot to make our base, and then we can stitch in and out of that room," said Amy.

Sister Margaret nodded. She undid the last little bit of her braid and massaged her aching scalp with her fingertips. "That sounds perfect. Let's do that. For now, we'll set a twenty-four hour watch over the door and record all comings and goings and whether each seems like something that's part of the routine or something that might be unusual. We'll turn the sound on too – see if the guards say anything interesting. What time is it now?"

Nicole checked her phone. "Quarter to two."

"Okay, so we'll watch until two o'clock tomorrow, in shifts," said Sister Margaret. "Then we'll plan our infiltration for tomorrow night. Sound good?"

There was a general murmur of agreement.

"I'll take the first watch," Giovani volunteered.

Sister Margaret nodded. "I'll take over for you in two hours."

Amy dropped her hand from Nicole's shoulder and the image on the wall disappeared.

Nicole stood up and Giovani took her seat, his eyes going white as he peered into the scrying stone.

Sister Margaret strode over to her suitcase and pulled out a tablet. She opened up her notes app and set the tablet on the table beside the scrying stone. "Use this to record anything interesting."

Giovani nodded without looking up.

Sister Margaret sighed. More waiting. Of course, it was best to plan these things out, and she knew that, but damn, did she hate waiting.

***

Much to Mattie's surprise – but not to Chameleon's – the communal computer in the convent library already had the browser needed to access the Dark Web.

"They're warrior nuns," said Chameleon. "Of course they use the Dark Web."

"Yeah, but, I mean, they're still nuns," said Mattie. "Isn't that a little sketchy?"

"Not necessarily," said Chameleon, absently as she typed in a web address. "Sometimes it's just more private."

"What are you looking for, anyway?" asked Mattie.

The website was taking a long time to load. That made sense; the computer was as ancient as advertised.

"A reason that Broken Bunker would be locked down to the point where only hallways are scryable," said Chameleon.

"So that's not standard?" asked Mattie.

"Of course not," said Chameleon. "Do you have any idea how much mage power that takes? It would be insane to have it like that all the time. There are a few spaces in the bunker that are always locked down. Father's chambers, a couple of library rooms with super sensitive materials, the detention wings...."

That caught Mattie's attention. "The detention wings? Tell me more about those. That's where Tillie and Trevor would be kept, right? Waiting for processing to turn them into good little agents?"

Chameleon looked at Mattie out of the corner of her eye. "They're not going to be processed. Not if they're in Broken Bunker."

"What, then?" asked Mattie.

Chameleon pursed her lips and inhaled sharply through her nose, still looking at her sideways.

Mattie narrowed her eyes. "What, then?" she repeated.

"They're probably going to be questioned. Tortured. And they are certainly scheduled to be executed."

6.

Tillie's chokehold on her sanity was growing weaker, and she could feel it, and the longer she held on, the more tenuous her grip grew. Her mind spiraled faster and faster, but still she held on, forcing her breathing to remain even, her body to keep moving.

Prowling through the bathroom, still naked as the jumpsuit dried, she located a hair dryer and a variety of other beauty tools in a cupboard so discreet she hadn't even realized it was a cupboard until she'd examined the protruding mirror closely.

They had given her a hair dryer, a curling iron, a variety of make-up and nail polish, but no underwear? There was something really weird about this place.

A high-pitched giggle escaped her lips, and she clapped a hand over her mouth, and closed her eyes, breathing deeply and forcing her thoughts into a more productive line.

There had to be a clue in all of this, right? Why give her these amenities? Why give her delicious meals, wine, and a luxurious shower? There had been no indication of what was coming.

Tillie plugged in the hair dryer and pointed it at the jumpsuit where it hung from the glass shower door.

She was growing more uneasy by the minute, and a seer knew not to ignore those feelings. This wasn't *just* anxiety. She needed to be ready for something to happen.

*****

Trevor collapsed into a brown leather easy chair. Ordinarily, he would have felt slightly guilty about bleeding on nice leather, but since the chair belonged to the Auditors and an Auditor had caused the bleeding, he was feeling pretty okay about that aspect of things.

He still wished he wasn't bleeding, of course.

Gingerly, Trevor lifted the blood-stiffened rag from the wound, twisting his head to see just how bad it looked.

It felt fucking awful.

The wound was still bleeding, but it had slowed considerably.

Trevor moved his right fingers into a stitching gesture, willing the flesh to close up.

Nothing happened and panic surged through him. He forced himself to calm down, knowing that if his heart rate escalated, it would just pump more blood out through the hole in his shoulder.

Breathing slowly and deliberately, Trevor made his stitching gesture again, and once more the knife wound failed to close.

"Come out into the hall," came a man's voice from the doorway.

Trevor jumped up and spun around, clutching the rag to his shoulder again, and stared at a man in the same scrubs-with-an-apron uniform that seemed to be the bunker's answer to chef uniforms.

"Get away from me!" Trevor yelled. With effort, he reached into his pocket with his left hand, and carefully grasped the only remaining glass shard.

Trying not to shake, he drew it out and brandished it at the newcomer.

"Relax," said the man. He lifted his hands in the universal sign for surrender. "I'm on your side."

"That seems likely," Trevor scoffed.

"You're Trevor, right?" said the man. "Lansdowne told me to watch for you."

Trevor's eyes widened as he recognized the name of the leader of the St. Louis Harpers, a group that had agreed to ally with his own group just before he'd been kidnapped. "Lansdowne did?"

"Yeah. And if you'll just come out into the hall, we can get that shoulder stitched up."

Trevor frowned. "What do you mean?"

"I don't know why, but magery doesn't seem to be working in most of the bunker right now; only in the hallways and a few other places."

"It worked in the kitchen," Trevor objected.

"Yeah, like I said, a few other places. We–" the man glanced up and down the hall and lowered his voice, "–the Harpers who are here – have a base that seems to be exempt for some reason too. If I can just get you to trust me, we can head that way. But the longer you hold out, the more you're just sitting there bleeding, and the more likely it'll be that someone will discover us, and I'll have to do something I don't want to do in order to maintain my cover."

As Trevor hesitated, he shifted position and his shoulder flared up in pain.

Stifling a howl, he nodded. "Fine," he said, through gritted teeth as soon as he could talk again. "Lead the way."

He stood up and made his slow way out into the hallway.

"Thank you," said the Harper. He hurried forward into the small library room and wrapped an arm around Trevor's mid-back to support him. "I'm Lewis, by the way."

"Thank you, Lewis," said Trevor.

They finally reached the door, and Trevor grabbed the frame, collapsing against it and rolling himself around the edge until he was leaning against the wall of the hallway.

"Okay," said Lewis. "Let's see what we're working with."

Trevor lowered the hand that held the rag and Lewis stepped forward to examine the wound. "You really did a number on Duchess Riley, you know."

"Good," said Trevor.

"No argument here," said Lewis. "She's a real fucking piece of work." He moved his hand into a stitch, identical to the one Trevor had been trying in the room, but this time Trevor's shoulder began to tingle, and after a few seconds, the pain began to diminish quickly.

A few more seconds and it had abated to a dull ache. He breathed a sigh of relief. "I'm so glad I was never stabbed in the shoulder before I discovered stitching," he said. "That was rough enough as it was."

"Glad to help," said Lewis. "But we need to get out of here. It's kind of astonishing that nobody has stumbled upon us yet. We need to get you changed out of that ridiculous prisoner uniform, and then rendezvous with my associate, who is doing some damage control in the kitchen right now."

He jerked his head and hurried down the hallway.

"We need to find my friend and get her out too," said Trevor as he followed close behind, trying to hurry despite the unpleasantly rough floor against his bare feet. "Do you know where Tillie is being kept?"

Lewis slowed a little, allowing Trevor to catch up and walk beside him. "One of the detention wings, for sure. We were trying to get one of us assigned to stitch the meals in and out, but of course you have to be subtle or they start getting suspicious, and we hadn't gotten there yet. As of this morning there are four prisoners here – well, I guess your escape puts it back to three. Agent Brown has been doing the meal delivery, but he's probably headed to the infirmary with a concussion. I think we can convince Count Biglow to give me or Doyle the job."

"And then they'll tell you where she is?" said Trevor.

"They'll give us the location of the three remaining prisoners, and then we'll have to check out each of them until we find her. Still, a one in three chance of getting her on the first try isn't too bad."

"Who are the others?" asked Trevor. "Shouldn't we rescue them too?"

"No idea," said Lewis. "I know they're not Harpers or Harper allies. They could be rogue agents, courtiers who pissed off someone higher up, or outsiders who found out about the organization but aren't considered good candidates for agenthood."

"I guess Tillie and I fell into the latter category," said Trevor. "What typically happens to people like us?"

Lewis' mouth twisted. "Nothing good." He suddenly stopped walking and turned to face Trevor. "It's not going to happen. We'll get her out. And there's an army heading our way. We'll take these guys out for good or we'll all die trying and then we won't care anymore anyway."

Trevor didn't find that super comforting.

***

"Executed? Tortured?" Mattie jumped to her feet. "We have to get in there! We can't just wait around for this army to be ready, for fuck's sake!"

"Relax," said Chameleon, waving a hand. "They're not being tortured yet. Remember? Lansdown's spies said there were two new prisoners and the timeline matched up with Tillie and Trevor's arrival."

"So?" Mattie stared at Chameleon.

"So, the spies are in the kitchen, right? They'd know if the prisoners were moved out of their cells; the main kitchens don't feed anyone in the torture chambers."

Mattie sat down heavily, studying the former Auditor spy. She had managed to forget for a while there who Chameleon really was.

Chameleon glanced in her direction and her expression softened slightly. "Things move slowly in the bunker," she said. She lifted her hands from the keyboard and swiveled her chair. "I've known prisoners to languish in the cells for months before being transferred to the torture chambers or put to death."

"How comforting," said Mattie. "Languishing in a cell sounds delightful."

Chameleon smiled. "Actually, you should see the cells in Broken Bunker. They're better than a lot of hotels I've stayed at. And the food is exquisite. Duchess Riley is a horrible person, but she's an amazing chef. Detainees get the same food as everyone else."

Mattie frowned. "Why?"

"Because," Chameleon pivoted back toward the computer screen. "Most of the people tossed in those cells are high court, and even high courtiers who have fucked up get treated like royalty." She grabbed the mouse and began to scroll through the message board on the monitor.

Mattie leaned forward. "What exactly are we looking for?"

"Hard to say," said Chameleon. "Special agents don't use a specific code; we just use mixed up languages and speak cryptically. Often messages are aimed at one Special or another, and we use what we know of that person's nature to code it just for them, rather than – oh, shit."

"What? Is it about them?" Mattie peered at the screen, but the jumble of languages was more than she could decipher. There was one line of English in there, but it was completely inscrutable to her: *Coyote under a salty smashed up tree. Buried. Could fly again?*

Of course that's the entry Chameleon pointed to. Fortunately, she was quick to translate. "I may have figured out why the bunker is locked down. Coyote is being held at Broken Bunker. Raccoon is asking if she should mount a rescue mission."

"Let me guess," said Mattie. "Coyote is a friend of yours."

"Coyote is my best friend." Chameleon's eyes widened as she kept reading. "It's interesting that Raccoon is interested."

"Is it?" said Mattie. "Why?"

"Because Raccoon is – fuck, fuck, fuck, fuck, fuck." Chameleon jumped to her feet and began pacing, her arms crossed, hands formed into claws, nails digging into the flesh of her arms as she raked them up and down.

Mattie leapt up after her. "Hey, breathe," she said. "What's going on? Are you having a panic attack?"

Chameleon stilled. Then, slowly and deliberately, she opened her hands and forced them to her sides, sucking in air and pushing it out again through clenched teeth.

"What can I do to help?" asked Mattie, softly. "Can I get you some water? Food? A blanket?"

Suddenly, Chameleon relaxed, throwing her head back and laughing merrily. "Oh, honey," she said, her voice two octaves higher and lilted like a Georgia peach. "Don't you fret yourself over me." She returned to the seat, a small smile playing over her face.

"Honey?" said Mattie, her eyebrows raising.

There was no sign of Chameleon's previous tension. "It's all just a misunderstanding, I'm sure," she continued.

"Okay," said Mattie. She sat down beside Chameleon and studied Chameleon's face. "What's a misunderstanding? Coyote being locked up?"

"Coyote's gonna be fine," said Chameleon. "We'll just have to mount a rescue, that's all. Nothing I can't handle with you by my side." Chameleon reached out and grasped Mattie's hand, giving it a companionable squeeze.

"Sure," said Mattie, extricating her hand. Since when was Chameleon so touchy-feely and into teamwork and friendship? It had to be part of this weird new character. "I mean, I'll do whatever I can. Should we join up with this Raccoon person?"

"Oh, I don't know that that's the way to go," said Chameleon. "I just never know from day to day what Raccoon is doing with her life. You know what I mean, honey?"

"I don't, actually," said Mattie. "I'd appreciate it if you could explain it to me."

"Well, she's just very changeable," said Chameleon.

Mattie had to bite back a hysterical laugh. Chameleon thought someone else was changeable?

"She's liable to switch sides at the drop of a hat," Chameleon continued. "And I can't be having someone like that on my side, less'n I'm absolutely positive about her, you know."

"Sure," said Mattie. "Makes sense. So, we're on our own, then?"

"Goodness, no," said Chameleon. "We've got all kinds of friends. And thanks to Coyote, looks like we're short a coupla enemies." She giggled. "Very efficient, that Coyote is. Always has been."

"So, who are our friends, then?" Mattie asked.

"Well, now here's the pickle," said Chameleon. "Look at this response here–" she pointed to a line of text beneath the English words, which were in some kind of Asian script. "There's something just a teensy bit off about it. But I can't quite put my finger on what it is."

"What does it say?" asked Mattie. She squinted at it, as though if she could just see it better, she'd magically be able to read the foreign language.

"Well, let's see, roughly translated, it's something like, 'Chicken broth can wait. We're cooking inside already.'"

"Well, that's helpful," said Mattie.

"Basically, I think Wolf is saying that he's already inside the bunker and things are heating up, and mounting a rescue isn't a priority," Chameleon explained. "Not that I'd generally trust Wolf as far as I can throw him."

"How did you get that from that?" said Mattie.

Chameleon shrugged. "I know these people. They're the only people I know." Her fingers hovered over the keyboard. "And they're the only people who know me, so I've got to be very careful before I post anything. They just may be able to read between the lines."

"You think they would figure out you've switched sides?" said Mattie.

Chameleon nodded. "You know, it could be advantageous if a coupla them know. So what could I post that, say, Rattlesnake, Meerkat, and Coyote – if he escapes – could read."

"But not Wolf or Raccoon?" said Mattie.

"Maybe Raccoon," said Chameleon. "Not Wolf. There's just– I don't know. Something about Wolf's message...."

Chameleon lifted her hand to her mouth and bit down hard on it.

Smelling blood, Mattie jumped up out of her chair. "Whoa, hey! Are you okay?"

Chameleon looked up, surprise written across her face. "What?" Her eyes followed Mattie's to her hand. "Oh, golly." She laughed shakily. "I hate it when I do that."

Pulling a roll of gauze out of her belt pouch, Chameleon returned her gaze to the computer screen, absently wrapped up her hand as she stared at the message board. "Chicken broth...." she mused. "I feel like that's gotta be significant. There are any number of other salty liquids he coulda used. Why chicken broth?"

"Chickens are associated with cowardice," Mattie suggested. She sat back down, eyeing the bandage around Chameleon's hand. But hey, if it didn't bother Chameleon, why should it bother her?

"Yeah," said Chameleon slowly. "But nobody would ever think o' Coyote as a coward. If anything, he's foolishly brave. Reckless, even." She twisted her head quickly, fixing Mattie in her intense gaze. "Gimme more things about chickens, would you?"

"Uhh," Mattie struggled to think. She and her ex-husband had had a coop with six chickens on their little farm. "They eat everything. They give you eggs. They have a pecking order. Roosters crow. You eat roosters and keep–"

"Stop!" Chameleon stared at Mattie, her deep brown eyes widening. She bit her lip and blinked several times. "I had it. What did I have?"

"Roosters?" Mattie suggested. "Eating?"

"YES!" Chameleon surged to her feet. "Chickens are food for Wolves and Coyotes."

"And Raccoons," Mattie pointed out.

"Yes," Chameleon crooned. She looked around and grabbed a small square of scrap paper and a golf pencil, as are found scattered around any library. "What else eats chickens?" She scribbled furiously.

"Lots of things," said Mattie. "The only things lower on the food chain are bugs and plants. It might be easier to list animals that you have in your group of codenames and then divide them up into chicken-eaters and herbivores, than to try and list all the animals that eat chickens."

"Right." Chameleon picked up another square of paper and set it down next to the first.

Mattie looked over her shoulder. Square one read *Wolf, Hyena*.

"Meerkats are vegetarians," said Chameleon, writing it down on the second square of paper.

"Rattlesnakes eat birds," Mattie pointed out. "You said Rattlesnake would be on our side."

"I said Rattlesnake would be on *my* side," Chameleon corrected. "And I don't think rattlesnakes are big enough to eat a chicken, are they?"

"I think they eat eggs, at least." Mattie pulled out her phone to look it up. "*A rattlesnake can eat a full-size chicken, but will rarely bother,* according to this."

"She's on our side," said Chameleon firmly.

Mattie noted the shift from *my* to *our,* but figured commenting on it would only distract from the task at hand. "Who else do we have?"

"Elephant," said Chameleon, writing it on the *friend* page. "And Bonobo. She's gotta be an ally, and a formidable one, at that. Hawk will undoubtedly be with Wolf, doncha think? Those two are hivey as hell."

"Hivey as hell?" asked Mattie. "What does that mean?"

"It's an expression among Specials," said Chameleon. "They are always together, always plotting, like ants or bees in a hive. And between you and me, they're always in each other's beds. Crocodile, too."

"They're a thrupple?" said Mattie.

"What's a thrupple?" said Chameleon, looking up with a frown.

"You know, a couple, but with three. Thrupple."

Chameleon grinned. "You mean a triplex. No, they're not. But I like that word. Is that a common word out here?"

Mattie shrugged. "I mean, I wouldn't say common, exactly, but people know it."

"Bless you, I love it." Chameleon shook her head and giggled. "Thrupple."

"I think we're getting distracted," said Mattie. "How many more do we have?"

Chameleon counted up the names on her two pieces of scrap paper and then added her own name and *Coyote* to the list of friends. "Six left – no, make that four. Cheetah, Weasel.... Weasel is a tricky one. Do weasels eat chickens?"

Mattie looked it up. "Yep."

"Grizzly and . . ." She trailed off. "Who am I forgetting?"

"Raccoon?" said Mattie. "You haven't written down Raccoon."

Chameleon looked troubled as her eyes met Mattie's. "I just don't know where to put Raccoon."

7.

Sister Margaret yawned as she watched the guards. They looked as bored as she felt, standing at attention in the tiny concrete box of an entryway chamber for hours on end.

She glanced at her phone. Not quite eight o'clock in the evening.

This particular group had been on duty for three hours and were starting to show signs of wear and tear.

So far, these guards seemed more disciplined than the last, who had leaned against the walls and joked around together.

These ones hadn't said anything to each other, except for once, an hour ago, when they had taken turns with a restroom break.

All of the guards wore the same bizarre orange midriff-baring uniform as the ones they'd seen with the court in St. Louis.

This group consisted of two women and one man, the women positioned on either side of the door leading out, while the man faced them, his back against the door that led into the bunker. The previous group had used the same formation, although that group had consisted entirely of women.

Sister Margaret had already recorded all of this in the notes app on her tablet, echoing the notes already taken by Giovani and Nicole before her.

A hand landed on her shoulder and she jumped up, whirling around, swords half drawn before she realized it was Amy.

Amy backed away, her eyes wide, her hands up in surrender.

Sister Margaret relaxed. "Sorry, *chica*. You gotta warn a person before you just sneak up like that."

Amy nodded. "You're right. I shouldn't have come at you from behind."

"You here to take over for me?" said Sister Margaret. She resheathed her swords and stepped back to let Amy take the chair. "Where is everyone else?"

"Down at the bar," said Amy. "Giovani thought it might be good to keep an ear to the ground, see if the locals have anything to say about the bunker or the organization."

Sister Margaret frowned. "I doubt they even know it exists."

"Well, there wasn't really anything else to do, right?" Amy sat down and turned her attention to the scrying stone.

"Fair enough," said Sister Margaret. "Guess I'll join them."

***

Tillie, clad once again in her striped jumpsuit, now with hair smoothed and straightened and a full face of makeup and feeling like herself for the first time in a while – no need to pretend to be Mattie here, after all – paced her cell.

The makeover had helped with the rising waves of panic, but she could still feel it there, just waiting for the tide to turn again.

Her stomach growled. She had never been as good as Trevor at tracking time, but she was pretty sure it had been longer than usual since she'd eaten.

Where was her dinner tray? Had she lost track of time or had the routine changed for some reason?

Tillie stopped her hand from reaching up to rake through her hair; she'd picked up that habit from Giovani, but there was no sense in ruining all the work she'd done on it.

She needed to *do* something, though. She could feel her breath begin to speed up again.

She pivoted on her heel and strode back into the bathroom to pull out a manicure kit and a small soaking bowl. She filled the bowl with warm water from the tap and took it into the main room, setting it down on the table a little bit more forcefully than necessary, splashing herself and the table.

Tillie stood still for a moment, breathing in. Breathing out. Counting to ten. Repeating until she felt her heart slow, her anxiety ebb.

Then she went back into the bathroom and pulled out the tray of nail polishes.

Selecting a deep purple shade, Tillie laid everything out on the table, and began to soak the nails on her left hand.

***

Trevor buttoned up the white dress shirt and eyed the sleek black jacket that was slung over the chair beside him. "I am definitely glad to be out of that coverall, but is the full three-piece suit really necessary?" he called.

Lewis poked his head into the small bathroom of the suite the Harpers had made their own. "Auditors don't do anything by halves – you know that. Now, you can't wear the kitchen uniform because the kitchen staff is small and people will know you don't belong. Harpers wear black suits, and enough of the agents like the whole Men in Black routine that we've managed to get away with wearing them while we're undercover too. I don't have anything else."

"I'm really more of a jeans-and-a-polo guy," said Trevor. At least they had also given him an unopened three-pack of boxer briefs. He supposed he could wear a suit, as long as he had proper underwear too.

"I'm sorry, but literally nobody else here is a jeans-and-a-polo guy," said Lewis. He leaned on the doorframe and looked Trevor over. "You'd stick out like a sore thumb. In this? You look great. Put the jacket on."

Trevor shrugged into the jacket and gave a little twirl. "Am I pulling it off? I feel like an idiot."

"Well, you look fantastic," said Lewis. "Formal attire suits you. No pun intended."

"Very little pun achieved," said Trevor.

"Bet you'd be a real killer in a tux," said Lewis. "Not sure if it's ladies or men you'd be killing – you're a hard one to read – but you'd knock 'em dead."

"It's neither," said Trevor. "But don't worry about it."

"All right, then," said Lewis. "Well, speaking of killing, let's get you all armed up and then see if Doyle's managed to figure out where Tillie is."

"No such luck." A rich feminine voice floated in from the central room. A tan, dark-haired woman dressed in the kitchen uniform strode in, stopping just inside the small bathroom and leaning against the wall.

Trevor recognized her and winced. "Sorry I tripped you back there in the kitchen."

"All good," she said. "That's just part of being undercover. Glad you didn't do anything worse." She undid her black apron and pulled it off, hanging it on a hook on the door along with another that probably belonged to Lewis. "The good news is that they're assigning me the task of stitching out the trays, but the bad news is that they refused to give me room specs, and they're waiting until tomorrow; not even going to give the prisoners dinner tonight."

"Oh, no," said Trevor softly, thinking of Tillie. He hoped she was holding herself together. She was one tough cookie most of the time, but every so often, her past trauma got the best of her and she cracked under pressure. Going hungry couldn't help.

"Yeah, well, more good news: they're getting us into the kitchen early tomorrow, and we're actually doing three hot meals," said the woman. She held out a hand to Trevor. "I'm Doyle, by the way."

"Trevor." He shook her hand. "So, what's the plan for tonight, then?"

"Sleep," said Doyle. She jerked her head. "Come on, I'll show you to your room."

8.

Sister Margaret sipped her Bud Light and listened to the chatter of her compatriots as they yakked about what they'd do with their lives once the job was done.

Even a little bit tipsy, they were careful of the words they used – nothing was said that couldn't have meant a simple contractual gig that they had all been hired to do.

Still, she nursed her beer and kept her ears open, listening to them, listening to other conversation in the bar, making sure nothing out of the ordinary was said by any party.

And a little bit of envy crept into her mind. She'd made the choice to give up her freedom, and it wasn't that she regretted it; but it would be nice to think about what she wanted to do next, instead of wondering where she'd be assigned.

Sister Margaret knew she was starting to outgrow her current post. This mission aside, there wasn't much for a WMP of her skills and training to do at a small convent in a mid-size city in America.

Before he'd headed back to the Vatican, Cardinal Neubacher had said as much to her.

"What are your ambitions?" he'd asked. "You can't think you'll be able to stay here much longer."

"I will do as my order sees fit," she'd said.

"And what if you had options within the Church as a whole?" he'd asked. "A woman of your talents might be able to choose among many prospects."

"I am a Sister of Saint Joan," she'd rebutted. "I will hold to my vows."

He'd lifted a hand. "No one is questioning your devotion to your vows. But perhaps the order could spare you. Think of it as a loan to another department within the Church. Maybe even a permanent loan.

You would still be serving the same cause. Is that something you'd be interested in?"

Damn straight, she was interested. But was it possible? Was it moral? Was it true to herself and the promises she'd made to herself, her family, and her God?

She wasn't naive enough to think that everything the Church did was on the up and up. Just because the offer was coming from a Cardinal didn't mean that it was a good choice.

Sister Margaret took another sip of beer and thought some more about what the future held for her.

***

"...and so if we can get these Special agents together and form a team, we may be able to help rescue Tillie and Trevor and Coyote and get things ready at Broken Bunker to prepare for the arrival of the army," Mattie finished. She looked expectantly at Sister Catherine and Father Sean. "What do you think?"

"We already have a team at Broken Bunker," Father Sean reminded them. "They are already there to rescue the prisoners and prepare ground for the army. Why do we need you there?"

Mattie opened and closed her mouth.

"Bless your heart," put in Chameleon, still doing the southern belle schtick. "We certainly wouldn't want to imply that your team isn't adequate. But my team and I know that bunker. We grew up there, we trained there, and we've lived there off and on between jobs."

Father Sean studied Chameleon, his eyes narrowing slightly. He opened his mouth, but Mattie interrupted before he could ask about the change in Chameleon's personality.

"Plus, they'd be undercover inside!" she interjected. "People inside know them and they would trust them with information!"

"Well, honey, I wouldn't go that far," said Chameleon.

"What?" Mattie stared at her. "Why not?"

"I mean, nobody really trusts the Specials, except maybe the high court, and let's face it, you killed off most of those bastards already anyway. And it's not like the Pontiff is going to tell us any information about where your friends are, even if he stooped low enough to learn that information."

"You're not helping," Mattie hissed.

Chameleon shrugged and stood up. "Look, we don't really need your permission, do we?"

Father Sean smiled gently and gestured for her to sit back down.

Crossing her arms, Chameleon lifted an eyebrow at him and remained standing.

"All right," said Father Sean. "You're right. You're both free women. Neither of you has sworn any vows to us or our cause. You could charge right in and do as you please. But without our knowledge or permission, you'll do more harm than good, if only by strewing chaos in our path."

Mattie sighed. "This Coyote person is her best friend," she said, softly. "And I think the Specials really would be valuable allies, if they're all as good as she is."

"How about a compromise?" Chameleon suggested. "We'll do it without your permission, but with your knowledge."

"What?" said Sister Catherine. "Please clarify that."

"We're going to Broken Bunker, Mattie and I," said Chameleon. "We'll meet up with the group already there. And we'll collect the Specials who are more loyal to me than to the organization. We'll infiltrate in advance of your siege. And we'll remain in contact with you the entire time, so you don't have to guess what we're doing. We're all working toward the same goal. But you're not in charge of us."

"Now, look–" Sister Catherine jumped to her feet, but before she could get any further, Father Sean grabbed her arm and guided her back into her seat.

"That seems reasonable," he said smoothly. "Let's make some plans. You can leave in the morning."

***

Tillie examined her nails and looked around her cell, exhaling deeply.

It didn't seem like she was going to be given dinner tonight. She hoped that meant there'd been some kind of upset with the organization, and not that they'd decided to starve her out.

Either way, there wasn't anything she could do right now.

With a yawn, Tillie stood up and wandered over to the bed. She put the manicure kit under her pillow – it wasn't as good as a real weapon, but some of those instruments could do some damage if she wielded them correctly.

Laying down, Tillie began some breathing exercises designed to help her sleep.

A few minutes later, she was snoring.

***

Mattie sat alone in the convent cafeteria, pushing her simple meal of kielbasa and veggies from side to side on her plate, her mind racing through the events of the day. She wasn't sure how it had happened, but she was no longer concerned that Chameleon was going to betray her and her allies.

Now she was concerned that Chameleon was starting to snap.

"May I sit?"

Mattie looked up, startled, to see Father Sean smiling benevolently at her from across the table holding a tray. "Yeah, sure." She gestured to the chair he was already pulling out.

"I think I can guess what's on your mind," he said. "Our young enemy-turned-friend, hmm?"

"I like Chameleon," said Mattie. "Against all odds and my better judgment."

Father Sean nodded and leaned forward, pushing his dinner tray back with his forearms. "I do too, and I think you and she make a good team."

Mattie perked up. "You do?"

"Absolutely. I also think, however, that she is a lot more fragile than she would like us to know."

"I have a theory, actually," said Mattie. "I've had a couple of students throughout the years who have exhibited similar behaviors."

"Oh?" Father Sean picked up his fork and took a bite of food, watching her expectantly as he chewed.

"I think Chameleon is on the autism spectrum," said Mattie. "And I think she's falling back on familiar patterns because she's overwhelmed right now, being in a situation she's never been in before."

"Interesting," said Father Sean. "She's used to donning and shedding characters and to being in high pressure situations. Right now she's expected to be herself and she hardly knows who that is."

Mattie nodded. "Plus, she's not doing anything here. She's just sitting around, wondering what her function is."

"Thus the need to go after her friend." Father Sean wiped his lips with a paper napkin. "It makes a certain amount of sense."

"I think she needs this," said Mattie. "She needs to be in a familiar situation, and for her a familiar situation is infiltrating a secret bunker."

"I suspect she can also do as she promises," added Father Sean. "If she can rally these Special agents and convert them to our cause, even just a few of them may be a valuable addition to our force."

"Agreed," said Mattie. She finally took a bite of her dinner. The vegetables didn't have much flavor, but the sausage was good.

"I'm glad we were able to touch base on this before you depart," said Father Sean. "I think you and Chameleon will do great things together."

9.

A loud BANG catapulted Trevor out of bed. He landed in a defensive pose, ready to kick somebody's ass.

There was nobody in the room, and he stood frozen, primed for action for a minute, until finally he took a deep breath and lowered his hands.

Cautiously and silently, he made his way to the door of his small bedroom and pressed his ear up against it. He could hear muffled voices – Lewis and Doyle were talking.

Trevor strained to listen more closely, trying to decide if he was hearing a third voice or if his mind was playing tricks. Maybe there was a magical way to amplify the voices?

It probably involved using seer magery, which he wasn't really comfortable enough with to try anything past just turning on seer sight.

He shrugged. He wasn't going to learn by waffling about it. Trevor concentrated on his eyes and used the inner voice he thought of as "mage voice," which sounded suspiciously like the stern voice his father had used anytime he'd been in trouble as a teen. He commanded his eyes to show him the voices out in the atrium.

He felt his eyes switch modes, and he could suddenly see an overlay of the future on top of the present. But he couldn't hear the conversation any more clearly.

Trevor sighed. Nothing seemed to be happening in the near future, so–

A thought meandered into his head. What if he could stitch the voices closer? He could stitch objects toward himself. Why not sound waves?

He switched his eyes back into normal mode and then closed them, looking within to find the perfect stitch. Trevor lifted his hands and instinctively made a gesture.

And suddenly he could hear the conversation clearly! His eyes popped open as he broke into a huge grin.

"–barely half-trained anyway," Doyle was saying. "I say we leave him here and go rescue the girl on our own."

Girl? Were they talking about Tillie? Was he the half-trained one? Trevor's enthusiasm waned.

"Come on," said Lewis. "You saw what he did to Riley. The guy's a bad-ass, trained or not. And he deserves to fight his own fight."

"Even if it could get him killed? Or us? I'm not a baby-sitter, Lewis. That's not what I signed up for."

Trevor frowned and made another stitch to cease the amplification. He'd heard enough. Opening the door, he strode out into the central room of the suite. "Is everything okay out here?"

"You heard me drop those books, huh?" said Lewis with a wry grin. "How'd you sleep?"

"Fine," said Trevor. He met Doyle's eyes. "I'm ready to rescue Tillie."

"We weren't sure you were going to get up," she said, a hint of challenge in her voice. Did she know he'd overheard?

"Well, there are no windows and I have no alarm clock, so how should I have known when to get up?" he asked, smoothly, his eyes still locked on hers.

She didn't respond, just narrowed her eyes without breaking his gaze.

"Oh, for–" Lewis stepped in between them. "Okay, okay. Enough of this pissing contest. Trevor, you must have heard us talking. Please forgive Doyle for doubting you; she doesn't know you and there will be plenty of opportunity for you to prove your mettle today. Doyle, you're outnumbered, as Trevor and I both think he should come along. Okay?"

Trevor nodded. "Okay. Just let me get dressed. And last night you mentioned weapons?"

"We have plenty to spare," said Lewis. "Meet back here in ten minutes. Is that enough time?"

"Yes." Trevor turned around and went back into his room. He had changed back into the coverall in lieu of pajamas the night before, but the black suit Lewis had given him was hanging in the closet, and he quickly changed, putting on the black slacks and white dress shirt.

He gave himself a look in the full-length mirror that was mounted on the back of the door. He liked the way the crisp white shirt looked against his deep brown skin, but he felt like an imposter in the stiff clothing.

Picking up the narrow black tie, Trevor struggled to remember how to tie it. After a couple of false starts, he managed and then he wrinkled his nose at the jacket.

Trevor hated jackets. They were so restrictive, and then there was that stupid convention of unbuttoning when you sit, buttoning it back up when you stand, an endless dance of button-unbutton-button. What was the damn point of it all?

With a sigh, he picked it up and put it on.

Looking in the mirror again, he suddenly stuck out his tongue and made antlers on the sides of his head with his hands. There. Now he felt like himself again.

With a grin, Trevor opened the door and strode out into the atrium to arm up.

***

Tillie woke up with a dull ache in her belly. Ordinarily, she would jump out of bed to greet the day, even imprisoned as she was.

This day didn't feel like it was worth greeting.

Rolling back over, Tillie snubbed the day and closed her eyes again. If there wasn't going to be any food, she might as well just sleep.

***

The morning air was already balmy as Mattie exited the high school gym and trotted toward the car they would take to Utah.

She stowed the backpack Father Sean had leant her in the already-open trunk of the beige Toyota Corolla that Chameleon had driven into the parking lot from . . . somewhere . . . earlier that morning. When Mattie had asked about it, the other woman had just shrugged and said, in her normal voice, "It's mine. We have need of it now, so I brought it here."

And that was that. Mattie was just glad they had a reliable vehicle and wouldn't have to take the bus across the country, as she'd done to get to St. Louis.

As she fussed with the contents of the trunk, rearranging everything already there to make the most of the small space – there was still a cooler of food and Chameleon's backpack to go in – Mattie saw someone walking toward her out of the corner of her eye.

Looking up, she was surprised to see Sammy. "Hey," she called out. "What are you doing here so early?"

He grinned and broke into a trot toward her. "Just hoping to get some extra training in," he said. "I've decided I'm definitely going with you guys to this bunker battle thing."

"Cool," said Mattie. She studied the trunk. There should be room for the rest now.

"What about you?" said Sammy. He gestured toward the trunk. "What's going on here?"

Chameleon appeared beside them, stooped over the cooler she had stitched with her. She stitched the cooler into the trunk and then disappeared again.

Sammy stared at the spot she had briefly stood, his eyes wide.

"We're heading west today," said Mattie. "Gonna meet up with some friends of Chameleon's, get them on our side." She examined Chameleon's placement of the cooler and decided it would do, even though it had ended up on the opposite side of the trunk from where she'd been planning to put it. Chameleon's luggage could go on the left instead.

"Today?" Sammy's eyebrows rose. "Who are these friends? More spies?"

"Yeah," said Mattie. "They all have animal names like her, and it sounds like they're all just as crazy."

"I love crazy!" said Sammy. "Take me along, please?"

Mattie turned to face him. "Take you? I thought you were trying to cram in more training before you leave."

"I'm cramming in more training so that Sister Catherine is more likely to let me come," said Sammy. "I'd rather just cut out the middleman and go with you. Besides, you can train me on the way. You and Chameleon are morphers. I want to learn to morph, not just spell."

Chameleon stitched in again, this time hauling her backpack. She shrugged it off and set it in the trunk, tucking it in between the cooler and Mattie's bag, rather than the spot Mattie had newly designated for it.

"What's going on?" asked Chameleon.

Mattie pursed her lips as she surveyed the car trunk. With everything scrunched in on the right side, it was just going to shift and spread out at the first sharp turn, and then everything would rattle around the whole trip.

"Can I come with you guys?" asked Sammy. "I'm like eighty-five percent sure that Sister Catherine is going to try and cut me out of the trip at the last minute if I wait to go with them."

Chameleon didn't say anything, and as the silence stretched, Mattie glanced over at the pair.

They were having some kind of staring contest – Chameleon's dark eyes boring into Sammy in a way that was probably meant to be soul-piercing, but Sammy was just standing there, hip cocked, arms crossed, eyebrows lifted, lips smirking, gazing right back.

Finally, Chameleon narrowed her eyes and jerked her head toward Mattie, eyes still fixed on Sammy's face. "It's Mattie's decision," she said. "I don't know anything about you."

Mattie shrugged. "You're an adult, right? You want to come, you can come."

Sammy's smirk stretched into a wide grin and he spun around, breaking Chameleon's gaze. "Amazing!" he proclaimed. "You will not regret this!"

"That's a very suspicious thing to say," Chameleon observed. "Nobody said anything about regret until now."

Sammy blinked, stilling his dance. "It's just an expression."

"Oh." Chameleon sighed. "Your expressions are all so different from the ones I know. I don't think I'll ever learn them all."

Mattie waved a hand at Sammy. "You. Get a pack like these from in there." She pointed to the heavy-duty backpacks in the trunk and then gestured toward the gym. "Take it home, pack it up, but not too full – just the essentials." Mattie paused, taking in Sammy's perfectly groomed appearance and stylish clothing. "And when I say essentials, I mean basic toiletries and one week of *practical* clothing."

Sammy's broad grin turned into a small, rueful smile. "I get why you said that, but I assure you, I can be practical, Mattie."

Mattie nodded. "Good. Be back here in–" she pulled her phone out of her pocket and glanced at the clock. "–thirty minutes?"

"Can do," said Sammy. He strode quickly into the gym.

"Is this wise?" asked Chameleon.

Mattie shrugged. "I don't know. I'm not really known for wisdom. But I do know that someone like Sammy is going to do what he's going to do, and it's better to have him in your sight than out of it."

Chameleon studied Mattie and nodded shortly. "You see yourself in him."

"Exactly," said Mattie. She inspected the trunk again. Sammy's pack would fit perfectly on the left. She wondered if Chameleon had known there would be another bag going in. Probably not. Either way – "We'll have to fit all of our weapons into one side of the back seat now," she pointed out.

"Then let's get packing," said Chameleon. She stitched herself out. Mattie opted to save her energy and walked into the gym instead.

***

Trevor sat very still on a stool against the wall of the kitchen, behind the small sight shield Lewis had erected around him.

The teenage sous chef – now in charge while Duchess Riley recovered from being stabbed in the eye – lectured Doyle on her new responsibilities as the head dishwasher while Agent Brown recovered from his own injuries.

"–and I expect the plates to be spotless," Count Biglow was saying, his skinny chest puffed up importantly. "I know they get sanitized after they're scrubbed, and I don't care. Duchess Riley's standards were high, and I intend to keep them until her return."

Trevor's attention wandered from the pompous teen's instructions.

Lewis was shredding zucchini at a stainless steel table in the middle of the kitchen, preparing for the omelets that were to be sent to the prisoners, since they'd missed dinner. He hovered a couple of inches off the ground, claiming knee pain and using the levitation spell to explain away the glowing hands caused by the shield hiding Trevor.

As Trevor understood it, breakfast was usually a more continental affair in the bunker, with pastries, cereals, yogurts, and suchlike made available to the general population in various breakfast nooks scattered throughout.

Prisoners, as he already knew, didn't typically get breakfast at all.

Trevor's left ankle began to itch, and he clenched his entire body in an effort to stop himself from scratching.

"–and of course you'll need to stitch the trays to the prisoners," said Count Biglow, at last.

Trevor's attention focused in on that and he forgot about his ankle. With great effort, he resisted his instinct to lean forward.

"Three remain, although I have every confidence that we'll find the other. Of course, once he's recaptured, he'll probably be sent straight to the torture chamber, and so he won't be our problem anyway."

Trevor suppressed a shiver.

Count Biglow picked up a piece of glossy photo paper from the table beside him. "Here are the rooms you will stitch the trays into." He began to extend the page, but snatched it back before Doyle could grab it. "You can stitch from a photo, can't you?"

Doyle nodded, her hand outstretched.

Count Biglow stared at her for a moment and then reluctantly handed the page over.

Trevor could see that there were four photos on the sheet, but couldn't make out any of the details on the images.

"Ignore the bottom picture," said Count Biglow. "That's the one that *Trevor* person was in."

The hatred in the count's voice when he said Trevor's name was palpable.

"Got it," said Doyle, her voice even. She examined the photos. "These are all pretty similar," she observed.

Count Biglow rolled his eyes. "There's a number on the wall of each room," he said. He began gesturing toward the photos. "And this one has the table against the wall. You can see the bed in this one is in a completely different position to that one, and this third one here has purple sheets on the bed. There are plenty of differences for you to fix on. Are you sure you can handle this, *agent*?"

It sounded like agents were almost as bad as Trevor in the sous chef's mind.

Doyle squared her shoulders. "Yes, sir."

"Good," said Count Biglow. He nodded and gestured toward the doorway that led into the dishwashing room, a clear dismissal.

Doyle disappeared through the door and Count Biglow bustled toward a large reach-in refrigerator, pulling out a clear plastic container full of cracked eggs and setting it down on the prep table.

Trevor's ankle began to itch again.

***

Sister Margaret slung the pack onto her back and shifted her weight from side to side, gauging its feel. She spun around quickly and drew her swords, thrusting them forward and then slashing them through the air.

"You're going to put someone's eye out," said Amy, looking up from her book.

"I'm aware of everyone's location," said Sister Margaret as she danced forward, swinging her swords around and around and then shuffling back, crossing her blades and then slashing them wide.

This pack would do nicely, and it contained supplies for a good week, longer if she needed to start rationing midway through.

"Have you packed for our journey?" she asked Amy. "We leave in a few hours, and we may be inside for several days or more. You'll need to be sure you can move about, run and fight with it on your back. Establishing a base right away may not be practical."

Amy sighed and set her tome aside. "No, I haven't. It's not my strong suit. Will you help me?"

Sister Margaret sheathed her swords. "It would be my pleasure."

***

Mattie started the Corolla and cranked up the air conditioning immediately. Living in the Pacific Northwest for the past fifteen years had completely ruined her tolerance for the heat and humidity of St. Louis.

It was only ten o'clock in the morning, for fuck's sake – the air had no business being this thick and heavy.

Sammy opened the back door and slid into the tiny square of the seat left empty after stuffing the rest with swords, knives, bows, arrows, and even a couple of axes. "Phew!" he said. "I hope it's cooler where we're going."

"It isn't," said Chameleon as she sat down in the passenger seat.

"Seatbelts," Mattie reminded everyone.

Chameleon clicked her seatbelt on without a word.

"Seriously?" said Sammy.

"Absolutely," said Mattie. "How would you feel if you didn't even make it to the battle because some shitsucker sideswipes me on the freeway and you weren't wearing a seatbelt?"

Mattie regarded Sammy in the rearview mirror until finally he sighed and pulled it down across his body. She waited until she heard the click and then shifted into drive.

***

Trevor's arms and legs were in grave danger of falling asleep by the time Count Biglow went into the walk-in freezer for a few minutes to grab a bag of hash browns.

As soon as the courtier left the room, Trevor was up off of his stool, shaking out his limbs and then stretching his back, neck, and face.

Quickly, before Count Biglow could return, Trevor dashed into the dishwashing room, and leaned against the wall, out of sight of the kitchen.

Doyle gave him a sidelong look as she loaded a rack of small plates into the large cube-like dishwasher and pushed the boxy cover over it to start the machine. "You doing okay?" she asked.

"How long was I sitting there?" Trevor moaned.

Doyle glanced at the clock over the doorway. "About fifteen minutes."

"Seriously?" A hufflike laugh escaped his lips. "That felt more like a fucking hour."

"Well, breakfast won't take too long to cook," said Doyle. "But we should wait until it's ready, so that your friend will have some food in her before going on the run."

Trevor nodded. "I hate to make her wait, but that makes sense. Another hour or two won't make a difference, but eating will."

"It won't be an hour," said Doyle. "Count Biglow will want to get lunch started soon, so he'll get breakfast done fast. Plus it's only three servings."

The dishwasher's sanitizing cycle clicked off, and Doyle lifted the cover.

Steam whooshed out, swirling around the rack of dishes. Doyle jerked her head toward it as she moved back to the sink and picked up another plate. "Might as well make yourself useful. Those plates go on that rack over there. Careful; they're hot."

Trevor tentatively touched one of the clean plates. It was warm, but not unbearable, so he quickly unloaded the rack and carried stacks of plates to the steel rack on the other end of the small room. He made three trips, depositing the stacks of six with a gentle clinking sound each time.

He could feel his body heating up quickly in the humid room, and the unaccustomed weight of the suit didn't help.

Trevor shucked his jacket, laying it over the seat of a stool identical to the one he'd occupied in the main kitchen and then rolled up the sleeves of his white dress shirt and moved the now-empty dish rack over to the stack of them near the door.

Doyle started the dishwasher again, and Trevor waited for another rack of dishes to put away, glad for something to do. Anything beat sitting perfectly still in the kitchen.

***

Tillie rolled over in bed again, desperately trying to ignore the gnawing feeling in her stomach. She had always been an active person, and her metabolism was not used to going this long without food.

It had been bad enough going without breakfast these past few days, but now that dinner had been skipped too, she was feeling queasy, empty, and depressed.

Speaking of queasy–

Tillie threw the covers off of herself and lurched to the bathroom, making it to the toilet just in time to empty her stomach. All that emerged was bile and saliva, and it left her feeling even worse.

She lifted her head from the toilet and leaned back against the bathroom wall, grabbing the end of the toilet paper roll and wiping her mouth without bothering to tear the squares off.

Her throat ached and her mouth felt like it was full of foul-tasting cotton.

Breathing heavily, Tillie pulled herself to her feet and staggered over to the sink. She turned on the tap and scooped handful after handful of water into her mouth, first swishing and spitting and then swallowing it down greedily once her mouth finally felt clean.

"Come on, Tillie," she murmured to herself. "You can survive without food, as long as you have water. You're going to be okay."

Something suddenly teased at her senses – that feeling she got just before an unexpected seer vision. Automatically, she waited, but no vision came through.

Of course not; she was in a spelled cell and magery wasn't working. This was just her innate sense that something was going to happen.

Tillie dabbed her lips daintily with a washcloth and then went back into the main room.

She stopped short in the doorway.

There was a tray of food on the table.

***

Trevor was back to sitting perfectly still on a stool, this time in the dish room as Count Biglow brought in each tray, after arranging it just so. It seemed odd how long he was spending on each one, considering his animosity toward Trevor, and the fact that all of these trays were going to prisoners.

Maybe it was simply a matter of professional pride, a need to fill the regular chef's consideral shoes.

As each tray came in, he would set it down on the desk beside the door, each time almost brushing up against Trevor on his stool.

Trevor held his breath whenever the boy was in the room.

Count Biglow set the tray down and stepped back to watch as Doyle flicked her fingers, sending each tray to its destination, starting with the cell pictured at the top of the glossy page. Then he went into the kitchen, fussed over the next tray, and brought it into the dish room, setting it down and watching again as it disappeared.

By the time the final tray was done, Trevor's body was aching again with the effort of keeping perfectly still.

"Good," said Count Biglow with a terse nod to Doyle once the last tray was gone. "Now, you'll wait one hour and then bring each one back."

He strode out of the room, calling out as he did so, "Agent Lewis! I need six quarts of onions julienned right now."

"Yes, chef!" came Lewis' voice from the kitchen. "Red or–"

Doyle turned on the dishwasher, drowning out Lewis.

Trevor jumped up off his stool. "Let's go!" he said. "I've been thinking, we should start with the last location, since my cell was at the very bottom and Tillie and I would have arrived at the same time."

"Makes sense," said Doyle. "You're on your own, though. Lewis and I have to stay here. We can't blow our cover by disappearing during a busy time of day."

"Wait, what?" Trevor blinked. "You're not coming with me?"

Doyle shook her head. "You'll be fine. All you have to do is stitch into the room, and if Tillie is there, stitch her out to our suite. If she's not, stitch back here and use the photo again to stitch to the next one until you find her."

"And what am I supposed to do with the other prisoners?" asked Trevor.

Doyle shrugged. "It should only take a second to glance around, see who is in there, and stitch back out. They won't have time to attack you."

"That's not what I meant," said Trevor. "Shouldn't we be rescuing them too?"

"Uh." Doyle opened and closed her mouth a couple of times. Apparently the idea had never occurred to her. "Why?"

Trevor stared at her. "Because they're prisoners. They've been kidnapped and are going to be turned into Auditor agents."

"Not these ones," said Doyle. "This isn't that kind of station. These ones are most likely courtiers who pissed off someone higher up than them."

Trevor thought about it for a moment. "Doesn't matter. I'm letting them out."

"You know that the most likely outcome of that scenario is that they'll immediately turn you in, in order to curry favor with the Pontiff," said Doyle. "Don't do it."

Trevor shrugged. "Maybe. That's up to them, not me. I have to do what I believe is right, and what other people do after my actions is their responsibility, not mine. I can't leave someone locked up, unless they're an actual criminal." He paused. "In fact, the United States prison system is pretty fucked up. If I had an opportunity to free actual criminals, provided they weren't violent, I would absolutely let them out too."

Doyle grabbed Trevor's arm. "I'm telling you, this is a bad idea. I can't let you do this."

"Not your decision," said Trevor. He picked up the photos and studied the one second from the bottom. "Besides, how the hell would I even stitch out of those cells? I can stitch in from here because magery works here. I'm going to have to cut my way out of the cells, so how would I do that and still leave the person inside?"

Doyle thought for a moment. "If the occupant isn't Tillie, then just incapacitate them and grab the tray. I'll stitch it back here after a few minutes. And if it is her, grab her hand and the tray. Again, I'll stitch the tray back a few minutes after you leave each time."

Trevor studied her. "Doyle, I'm sorry, but that isn't going to work for me. I'm rescuing whoever is in that cell. Hopefully it's Tillie, but even if it isn't, I simply cannot leave them there."

"Dammit, Trevor, you're making a mistake!" said Doyle. She tried to rip the page from his hand, but he held on tight, and she only succeeded in tearing off the top image. "If you do this, you're on your own. I'm not stitching you back out!"

She reached for his hand to seize the rest of the paper, but Trevor stitched himself out before she could, and found himself in a cell similar to the one he had recently occupied, but for a few small details.

He looked around, but it seemed to be unoccupied. Looking at the table, he saw that the breakfast on the tray was half eaten.

Trevor turned around slowly and stared at the closed door to the bathroom, just as he heard the sound of a toilet flush.

10.

Sister Margaret propped her head up on her hand, willing herself to stay awake as she stared into the scrying stone, watching the guards doing absolutely nothing. Still.

She felt her eyelids begin to droop. Again.

That was it. Sister Margaret jumped to her feet and addressed her startled comrades as they looked up from books and maps. "This is getting ridiculous."

"It was your plan," Giovani pointed out.

"And I'm revising it," she said. "There's no need to watch for twenty-four hours. We've learned what we need to learn. The guard changes every six hours. Nothing else happens ever. So, if our plan is to jump in right after the guard changes, that'll be in about twenty minutes. We should just leave now. We're all packed up already. There's no need to wait."

"Sounds good to me," said Nicole, scrambling to her feet. "Let's drive out to the door; the shorter the stitch, the better."

Sister Margaret zoomed out on the scrying stone, studying the outside of the door. "Looks like there are tracks here – not a road, exactly, but cars do drive right up to the entrance."

"Those fancy buses the court takes everywhere, probably," said Amy.

"Let me see," said Giovani, flipping his eyes into seer mode.

Sister Margaret stepped aside for him to use the stone.

"Yeah," he said, after a moment. "I think the SUV can handle that."

"Let's hit it," said Nicole, her pack already on her back.

Sister Margaret grabbed her own bag and led the way out the door.

***

In a rest stop along I-70, just shy of Kansas City, Mattie walked in a lap around the building, glad to be out of the car and able to stretch her legs.

As she reached the end of her orbit, she looked around for her companions. Sammy was a little ways off, doing tai chi or something similar on a patch of grass.

Chameleon was nowhere to be seen – probably using the restroom, which was next on Mattie's agenda as well. She headed in that direction.

Stepping into the dank and musty women's room, Mattie avoided clumps of toilet paper and a suspicious puddle in the middle of the floor. She made her way to one of the three stalls and then frowned. Chameleon wasn't in here either.

She shrugged. Honestly, if Chameleon betrayed them, there wasn't much Mattie could do on her own, and Sammy wasn't going to be a huge help either.

Might as well just assume she was trustworthy.

Mattie completed her business and washed her hands. She waved her hand in front of the automatic towel dispenser, but nothing came out. As she bent down to peer into it, she spotted a stack of paper towels on the counter next to the sink.

Feeling slightly foolish for missing that, Mattie grabbed a couple and dried her hands, wondering as she did so why they had bothered to put up a "mirror" that was just a polished piece of scratched up metal. Nobody could possibly see enough of themselves in there to be helpful.

She reached for the door, but before she could grab the handle, it swung open and Chameleon walked in.

"Oh, there you are," said Mattie. "I was looking for you a minute ago."

"I had some calls to make," said Chameleon.

"You have a phone?" said Mattie. She'd never seen her use it.

"Of course I have a phone," said Chameleon. "It's the twenty-first century." She pulled out an old-fashioned flip phone and waved it around.

"That's your phone?" Mattie's eyebrows shot up. "You know it's the twenty-first century, right?"

Chameleon frowned. "Yes, I just said that."

"Yeah, I know, but– never mind. Who were you calling?"

"We never posted a response to Raccoon's message," said Chameleon. "And I thought it made more sense to reach out individually anyway, instead of trying to tailor one message to read differently to different people."

"Fair enough," said Mattie. "I didn't realize we had that option."

"It's not done very often," said Chameleon.

The door opened and a frazzled young mother shooed in two toddlers.

Mattie and Chameleon gave the family identical tight smiles, which the mother returned before herding her children into the large handicapped stall at the other end of the room.

"I'll meet you outside," said Mattie, pulling open the door. She walked out and the heat smacked her in the face. "Ugh. I hate the midwest," she muttered.

She pulled her water bottle out of her cross-body purse and took a healthy swig as she wandered over to a nearby bench to wait for Chameleon.

A man walked by with a cat on a harness.

"Oh, shit," she muttered. "Tillie's cat!"

Mattie thumbed through her phone contacts, hoping she had the number for Tillie's next door neighbor who had taken care of Max before. She did have it, so she shot off a quick text, asking him to help out.

A response came through almost immediately. The cat was already in his care; Tillie had enlisted his assistance before she'd been kidnapped because she was out of the condo so much.

Mattie breathed a sigh of relief.

Chameleon sat down beside her. "So, I was able to talk to a couple of people and left messages for a few others."

"Who did you talk to?" asked Mattie. "People squarely in the friend column?"

"Yes," said Chameleon. "And also Raccoon. I'm . . . still not sure about her."

"What did you say to her?" asked Mattie. "She won't suspect anything about you, will she?"

Chameleon shook her head. "I was careful. I told her that I had been captured, that I am now free, and waited for her to bring up Coyote."

"And what did she say?" Mattie took another swig of water. On the one hand, she wanted to head back to the car and turn on the air conditioning. On the other hand, she was enjoying the ability to stretch out her legs in front of her.

"She's in La Panne, not at the bunker, but in the nearest town–"

"Wait, La Panne is the nearest town to the bunker?" Mattie interrupted. "What are the odds?"

Chameleon raised an eyebrow. "You're familiar with La Panne, Utah? Population seven hundred humans, and about a thousand goats?"

"I don't know if familiar is the word," said Mattie. "But my car broke down there while I was driving out to St. Louis in May. I ended up leaving a bunch of my stuff with a mechanic there after he bought the car to strip for parts and then dropped me off at the bus station in Salt Lake."

"What mechanic?" said Chameleon sharply, her whole body going still.

"Um. Jorge something, I think?" said Mattie. "Why?"

Chameleon's lips curved and she chuckled. "Jorge Gonzales? That's Coyote. Coyote and Wolf were stationed undercover in the town as mechanics. You left your things with Coyote."

"What about the other guy I met?" said Mattie. "Johnny, he said his name was, and he was a seer – I saw his eyes go all white, and at the time I didn't know what was happening and it freaked me the fuck out."

Chameleon shrugged. "Doesn't ring a bell. Most of the people in the town aren't connected with the organization. We know there is a Harper or two there to keep an eye on the bunker, but other than that, we believe everyone to be completely ordinary." She paused. "Anyway. Back to Raccoon. She asked if I had any information. I told her I didn't. She asked if I was going to mount a rescue, and I countered, asking if she knew what he was locked up for. She said he'd been caught conspiring with Harpers and was scheduled for the torture chambers for next week."

"So, maybe Johnny is one of the Harpers," Mattie mused. "The two of them seemed to be on pretty friendly terms."

"Maybe." Chameleon shrugged. "Just because he's a mage doesn't mean he's connected with a secret society. My understanding is that most mages aren't, after all."

"Huh. It feels to me that they are, but I suppose I've had a pretty unusual introduction to the whole mage thing," said Mattie.

"The thing is, though," Chameleon continued. "I don't know how Raccoon would know the schedule. It's her job to know the why, but the when? That feels like phishing."

"Maybe she figured it out so she would know how long she had to rescue him," said Mattie.

"Could be," said Chameleon. She pursed her lips and shook her head. "It's not worth speculating, honestly. We just need to make a decision: to trust Raccoon or not. It's basically a 50/50 gamble at any time."

"Wow," said Mattie. "That is hard. What about the other people you talked to?"

Chameleon brightened. "Yes! Bonobo and Elephant are both on board. We actually need to make a slight detour in Colorado, in fact, to pick up Elephant."

Mattie glanced at the packed backseat of the car. "How are we going to fit another person in there?"

"It's just Elephant," said Chameleon. "She'll fit."

Mattie's eyebrows shot up. "That seems counterintuitive."

Chameleon shrugged.

Sammy wandered over to their bench. "Is this our new home?" he asked. "Are we staying here forever?"

"Point taken," said Mattie. She pulled the keys out of her purse and tossed them to Chameleon. "Tag, you're it."

Chameleon caught the keys and looked at them, then looked at Mattie, and then back at the keys. "I don't get it."

"Don't worry about it," said Mattie. She led the way back to the car. "You're driving."

***

Trevor situated himself beside the bathroom door, hoping to duck behind it as whoever was in there exited.

Unfortunately, the bathroom door in this cell swung inward.

A short young man with copper skin, a floppy mop of black hair, and an open, good-natured face strode out of the room, sat down at the table, and picked up his fork. He wore the same style of striped jumpsuit that Trevor had before he'd escaped.

Trevor froze. He pressed himself up against the wall as though that would make him somehow invisible.

The guy at the table cut off a bite of omelet and scooped it up. He paused with the fork halfway to his mouth. "Why don't you join me? I don't think I can enjoy this with you standing there staring at me like a scared rabbit." Without turning his head, he finished his bite and lowered his fork.

Trevor stepped forward cautiously, arms up and ready to move into a krav maga fighting stance at a moment's notice.

"What's your name?" asked the man. "And do you have anything to do with this whole no-dinner-sudden-breakfast situation?"

"Ah." Trevor cleared his throat and lowered his hands, gripping the back of the chair opposite the young man. "Trevor. And yes, actually."

A tiny smile tugged at the man's lips. "So, you're shaking things up, huh?" He studied Trevor for a moment as he took another bite, chewed, and swallowed. "You're dressed like a Harper, but I get the feeling you're not used to it. And you're using your first name – Harpers use their last. You could be newly escaped and inducted into the Harpers, but then you'd probably be calling yourself 'Agent' still. Plus there's no way they'd trust a new recruit to infiltrate the bunker. . . ."

Trevor opened his mouth to explain, but the man held up a hand to forestall him.

"No, no, I'll get it." He snapped his fingers. "You're with that new group! The Foxes! I heard you all were reclaiming your first names, right? Am I right?" He broke into a huge grin. "I'm right, aren't I?"

"Sort of," said Trevor. "I mean, I'm with the Foxes, but I was never an Auditor, so I've just always used my first name."

The man's grin widened. "Holy shit, you're *that* Trevor?" He dropped his fork and extended a hand. "It is a pleasure to meet you, sir. The name's Coyote, and I am very much at your service."

Trevor blinked, but automatically shook the man's hand. "Your name is Coyote? No title? No duke or count or agent?"

"Well, if you want to get technical about it, it's Special Agent Coyote or Jorge Gonzales, Baron of Perimeter Security for Broken Bunker."

Trevor pulled out the chair and sat down. His fingers were still at the ready to stitch himself out if need be, but Coyote had a way about him that was really putting him at ease.

"You're an agent, but also court?" he asked. "How'd you pull that off?"

"Special agent," said Coyote. "I'm a spy."

"Like Madeleine," said Trevor.

Coyote frowned. "Who?"

"She infiltrated our group as Agent Shezza and then again as Polly," said Trevor. "We put her under a spelled truth serum and found out her real name is Madeleine."

Coyote studied Trevor with narrowed eyes. When he finally spoke, his voice was flinty and hard. "Her *real* name is Chameleon. Madeleine is her birth name, but she's never used it. You put her under a truth spell? What else have you done to her?"

Trevor held up his hands. "Hey, whoa. I didn't do anything to her, personally. And if it makes you feel any better, I was not happy about the truth serum either. Anyway, she's with us now, so it must not have been that bad." He realized, as the words left his lips, that he didn't know anything about this guy, and hoped he hadn't said anything that would put Madeleine – Chameleon – in danger. Too late now, if he had. He met Coyote's light brown eyes.

Coyote gazed back, studying Trevor's face. He reached forward and took a sip of an orange beverage in a champagne flute – a mimosa from the looks of it.

Trevor's nostrils flared and his eyes narrowed as he lifted his chin, still staring into Coyote's eyes.

Finally Coyote began to laugh. "You've got moxie, Trevor, I'll give you that. So. If I understand you correctly, Chameleon has finally gone rogue. Delightful. I've been trying to convince her to do that for years."

"What about you?" said Trevor. "I take it you've also gone rogue? Is that why you're here?"

Coyote shook his head. "Oh, I've always been rogue. I'm here because I got caught. My fucking pops turned me in. He's always been a real bastard. Has a ridiculous hard-on for the notion of getting promoted out of the ranks of Special agents and into the regular high court. Like that would make him happy." Coyote drained the rest of his mimosa. "He's got blinders on; has no idea what high court is like. Not that I have any first-hand knowledge, but anyone with eyes can see that those courtiers are constantly bickering, looking over their shoulders, just waiting for someone to come along and assassinate them if they don't do the assassinating first. Honestly, that's where the real power is – become a high court assassin. Of course, your lot killed all of those guys in St. Louis, so I guess the joke is still on them."

Trevor's brain was starting to hurt. "So, let me get this straight. You're a spy. Your dad's a spy. You like being a spy, but your dad doesn't. But you're a rogue spy. And your dad reported you so he could curry favor with the high court and get to stop being a spy."

"That's about the long and short of it," said Coyote. "Now. Let's get back to you. What are you doing here?"

"Looking for my friend, actually," said Trevor. "But I guess I got the wrong cell."

"And where do we stand on you breaking me out of here, even though I'm not the one you were looking for?" asked Coyote.

"That's the plan," said Trevor. "Although Doyle told me not to."

"Doyle?" said Coyote. "Harper, right? Tall woman? Kind of a biracial look to her?"

"That's Doyle," said Trevor.

"She's a smart one. You probably shouldn't go around springing just anyone loose from these cells." Coyote finished his omelet and pushed the tray back. "But I do think you should make an exception for me. Out of curiosity, what is the plan to break out?"

Trevor pulled a small, but sharp serrated knife out of a sheath in his left boot and then another from his right boot. "Lewis gave me these and said they'll cut through the drywall."

"You're very familiar with the local Harper contingent, aren't you?" said Coyote.

"You're surprisingly familiar with them yourself," said Trevor, "considering they never mentioned you."

"It's my job to know what's going on with them. It's also my job to stay off their radar," said Coyote.

"But you're not doing your job," Trevor pointed out. "You went rogue."

"Going rogue is tricky," said Coyote with a grin. "You still have to do your regular job or people get suspicious. But you do just enough of it to not do too much harm, and you sabotage just enough to keep the Man off your back."

"So, what did you sabotage?" asked Trevor.

Coyote's grin faded. "Don't worry about it."

Trevor's eyebrows rose. "You know that just makes me wonder more."

"Sorry." Coyote got to his feet. "Enough chit chat. Let's get to sawing, shall we?"

He held out his hand and Trevor put one of the knives in it, handle first.

"Any idea which wall leads to the hallway?" he asked.

"It's always the one with the room number on it," said Coyote. He stepped over to the wall and pushed the pointed tip of the knife into it.

Trevor joined him and together they began to cut a doorway.

**

Sister Margaret braced herself on Amy's shoulder as she dealt with the moment of disorientation that she always felt when being stitched. She hated that feeling, but was quick to recover, stepping away from Amy and drawing her swords just a split second later, as the guards were still reacting to their sudden appearance.

Nicole threw a spell at the panic button and it exploded into a shower of sparks.

Satisfied that that was taken care of, Sister Margaret spun gracefully to meet the attack of one of the guards, a large man whose weapon of choice was a double-headed ax.

That struck Sister Margaret as an incredibly impractical weapon to be using in such a tiny space.

Easily trapping the ax-head between her swords, she kicked him backward toward Nicole, who was now looking around for an opponent.

Nicole slit the man's throat and spun around to face a svelte woman dancing toward her with a stiletto knife.

Sister Margaret jumped toward Amy, who looked cornered by her opponent, but as she did so, Amy turned the tables, slashing across the woman's bare midriff with her short sword.

Turning back toward Nicole, Sister Margaret watched as the guard crumpled.

"So, that's everyone, then," said Sister Margaret, sheathing her swords. "That was . . . suspiciously easy."

"Where's Giovani?" asked Nicole with a frown.

"Shit." Sister Margaret hadn't even registered Giovani's absence. "He was supposed to stitch himself in, right?"

"Yeah," said Amy. "I stitched you in, Nicole and Giovani were stitching themselves."

"He's not an extremely strong stitcher," Nicole observed. "But there shouldn't have been any issues with just himself and at such a short distance."

"Well, he'll just be right outside, then, right?" said Sister Margaret. She turned to the door that led out of the bunker. "Let's just ask him what happened."

Grasping the door handle, she pushed and then pulled, but both methods proved ineffective. "Is it locked?" she asked. "The handle turns fine."

"Let me see," said Nicole.

Sister Margaret stepped aside and Nicole examined the tight-fitting crack around the door. "I don't see a deadbolt."

"It must be a spell," said Amy.

Sister Margaret tried to turn her eyes to seer mode, but nothing happened. She let out a stream of curse words in mixed English and Spanish. There were some situations in which one language simply wasn't enough. "Okay, so there's a spell preventing any magery in here," she said. "That doesn't explain why he didn't stitch in from out there. Obviously the spell didn't prevent stitching, because we're here."

Nicole pounded on the door. "Giovani?" she called. "Can you hear us?"

Someone pounded back, and a muffled voice came faintly from behind the door.

"What's he saying?" asked Amy.

"I can't make it out," said Sister Margaret. She pulled out her cell phone. "One bar. I probably can't call him, but a text might go through." She began typing quickly, and then hit send.

After a moment her phone dinged and she read the text aloud. "'I was about to stitch in, but my backpack wasn't sitting quite right, so I was a moment behind you. It's not working now. I can't get in.'"

"I wonder if there was a dead man's switch connected to the panic button," Nicole speculated. "And it triggered a spell to prevent stitching in."

"That's always a possibility," agreed Sister Margaret. "If that's the case, then they're also aware that we're here, and we can't stick around." She shot off another text to that effect to Giovani and then stowed her phone back in its pouch on the bandolier across her chest. "Come on. Let's get moving. We're down one, but at least it's not because he's dead."

***

Giovani stared at the round wooden door in frustration. There was no handle on this side to even try. And it glowed brightly with layers of spells in his seer vision.

He switched off his seer sight and focused on picturing the antechamber in his head – again. He moved his fingers in a stitch – again – but nothing happened. Again.

It was clear that he was stuck outside, and there was nothing to do right then but drive away.

He opened the driver's door of his SUV, and took off his backpack, flinging it into the interior with more force than was necessary.

Why had he stopped to adjust the pack?

If he had just stitched himself into the bunker at the same time as his companions, he wouldn't be in this mess. He'd be in whatever mess the rest of them were in, which was probably something.

After all, life was pretty much one mess after another.

Giovani slid into the car and started it, revving it viscously. "Was there ever a time when my life wasn't a fucking mess?" he growled to himself as he savagely wrenched the gear into reverse.

There was a time, actually. He knew that. And that time had ended when he got himself kidnapped and turned into an agent of the Auditors.

"No," he said out loud. He slowed down, taking the gravel road a little more carefully. "You know what? I didn't get myself kidnapped. They kidnapped me."

He was firmly against anyone else feeling guilty about crimes perpetrated against them; why was he so quick to victim-shame himself?

He had done nothing wrong, nothing that was hurting anyone else. The organization's rules were designed with one purpose – to keep other mages from becoming as powerful as they were.

And he had dreamed big, come to their attention, and been stomped on.

"Not my fault," he murmured.

He stopped at the intersection with the state highway and looked both ways. It was deserted, so he turned towards town.

"Get back to the motel, regroup, stop blaming yourself, and figure out how you can help get Tillie back," he told himself. "And Trevor," he added.

It wasn't that he didn't care about Trevor. But he had feelings for Tillie that he couldn't deny and the thought of her going through the same shit he'd been through was making him crazy in a very inappropriate and caveman-like way.

Not that Tillie needed his protection. Nor would he be as into her if she did. Damsels in distress had never been his style.

He pulled up to the motel a few minutes later and turned off the car. Somehow he couldn't bring himself to get out of the car. His limbs felt heavy and he just sat there, staring at the door to their room.

Finally, he shook his head, reached over to grab his pack, and headed into the room.

Shutting the door, he took his phone out of his jacket pocket. Best thing to do first would be to see if he could contact the group inside again. He suspected not – they were in an underground bunker, after all, and once they moved on from the antechamber, would undoubtedly be out of reach of cell service.

He typed in a text, asking them to respond if they received it.

Next would be to contact allies elsewhere, and see if they had any ideas of how to break in. He'd text Mattie; last he'd heard, she and Shezza – oops, Chameleon, she was going by now – were heading his way.

Chameleon was probably their best bet for someone who could break in. If nothing else, he could join forces with them once they arrived.

Giovani sighed as he stared at the silent phone, willing it to make a noise. Nothing happened; either they were busy or out of range. Either was equally likely.

Feeling kind of silly standing in the middle of the room, Giovani took his jacket off and tossed it on the nearest bed, then sat down on the bed beside it.

He loosened his tie and thought about what to say to Mattie.

I got separated from the group. I'm back at the motel, and they're inside the bunker. Can you help me get in? he typed. He read it over and hit Send.

He took off his brown dress shoes and swung his legs onto the bed, scooting back to lie down with his head on the pillow.

As he waited for a response to either text, his eyes began to drift shut.

***

Trevor followed Coyote out into the hall, ducking and squeezing through the narrow rectangle they had cut.

"Ahhhhh," said Coyote, spreading his arms in the hallway. His hands began to glow and his jumpsuit turned from striped to black. "What a delight to be back in civilization."

Trevor looked at him sideways. "A hallway in a bunker in the middle of nowhere is 'civilization' to you?"

"Anywhere I'm not behind a shield that prevents me from using my magic is civilization," said Coyote. "It's best to have low standards so as to not be disappointed."

"Fair enough," said Trevor. "That's not something I've ever been good at, but I can certainly see the benefits. Did you actually just change your clothes or is that an illusion spell?"

"Illusion," said Coyote. "But it would still be best to find something else to put on before we proceed to finding Tillie's cell." Without further ado, he spun around and grabbed Trevor's arm with his left hand. His right moved simultaneously in a stitching motion.

Trevor looked around at his new location, a small bedroom about the size of the prison cells. This room, however, looked like it belonged to someone.

Even the suite the Harpers had taken over had a hotel room vibe, but this room – this room was lived in.

The walls were covered in an off-white wallpaper with a pattern of paw prints traversing it diagonally every six inches or so. Scattered across the walls were framed candid photos of people. Trevor noticed that Coyote was in several of the pictures.

He stepped closer to one, recognizing the woman Coyote had his arm around, standing in front of a stone pub with climbing roses growing all around the door. "She looks happy," said Trevor.

Coyote glanced up from the dresser he was rummaging in. "Chameleon? Yeah, she does, huh? That's a rare and precious moment there." He stepped forward to stand next to Trevor and draped an arm over his shoulder, leaning close to examine the picture. "Two years ago. Scotland. We were tracking this seer who was formerly married to an agent and had been trying to find her after she'd been brought in. He was good. He almost found her."

Coyote pressed his lips together and inhaled sharply, nostrils flaring. "I couldn't talk her into letting him go that time," he said, softly.

"That time?" said Trevor. "So, you've let people go before?"

Coyote dropped his arm and straightened his back, breaking into a wide grin. "Whenever I can, friend. Whenever I can. And Chameleon has been getting better about that too. I'm an excellent influence on her, you know."

He returned to his dresser, which was strewn with more photos intermingled with crystals, jewelry, feathers, coins, and a large scrying stone.

Crow might be a better name for the man – he was clearly fascinated by shiny things.

Coyote pulled several garments from the drawers and without a moment of hesitation, pulled off the jumpsuit he was wearing.

Trevor politely turned his back, examining more of the photos, which seemed to have been taken all over the world. There were a few more with Chameleon in them, but none in which she looked quite as happy as she had in Scotland.

"Okay," said Coyote behind him. "I'm just going to use the restroom again, and I suggest you do the same. You never know what'll happen in a rescue mission and when a bathroom will be available again. Have you eaten?"

Trevor shook his head, feeling a little bit like a small child about to go on an outing to the park or something. He turned around to address Coyote, who was now dressed in a new jumpsuit, this time a mechanic's black canvas coveralls. "Haven't had a chance today."

Coyote's eyebrows shot up. "Well, that's not good. It must be pushing lunchtime by now." He picked up an old-fashioned pocket watch from among the junk on top of the dresser. "Past lunchtime," he observed. His habitual mischievous smile grew. "I guess they'll figure out I'm gone when they stitch my lunch tray back and it's untouched. In the meantime–" He knelt down in front of a white minifridge, shoving aside a stack of dirty laundry in order to open it up. "It's been a minute since I've stocked this, but . . . here. This should still be good."

Trevor accepted a pint of peach yogurt. He moved his fingers in a stitch, trying to grab a spoon from the dish room off the kitchen.

"Oh, you won't be able to stitch in here," said Coyote. "You haven't got the credentials." He held out his hand and stitched a spoon into it, handing it to Trevor. He stitched a bottle of water into his other hand

and gave that to Trevor too. "Now, eat up, use the bathroom, and then we'll go rescue your friend. And then maybe the three of us can wreak some havoc."

***

Mattie stared out the window, mesmerized by the endless fields of corn streaking past the car, broken occasionally with a field of soybeans or a farmhouse. Kansas was not her cup of tea.

"I can't look at this another minute," she muttered. She glanced at Chameleon, whose eyes were fixed on the road as she drove. She seemed pretty in the zone, and didn't seem to notice Mattie's words at all.

Snores drifted forward from the back seat where Sammy dozed.

Mattie leaned forward and pulled her phone out of the front pocket of her purse. About to open up her library app to see if she could find a good ebook to get into, she paused.

"Oh, shit," she said. "Missed a text from Giovani."

"What's it say?" asked Chameleon, her voice absent.

Mattie clicked through and read the text. "Oh, shit," she repeated. "Sent a couple hours ago. I guess the main group is in, but Giovani got separated and can't seem to stitch in."

"Mmm," said Chameleon. "If he was behind the others and the lockdown protocol happened, he'd be stuck, yeah. At least until we get there."

"We can get him in?" said Mattie.

"Of course," said Chameleon. "Tell him to hang tight and then he can join us on our mission instead."

Mattie relayed the message and waited, but nothing came back. She opened her library app and started looking for something funny to distract herself.

***

Sister Margaret prowled the doorless hallway, examining every feature of it as Amy led them toward the out-of-the-way library room they were planning to use as their home base while inside.

She felt blind without her seer abilities. She couldn't blame the Auditors for dampening magery in the bunker, although she couldn't help but wonder how it wasn't just as inconvenient for them as for her.

They must have some kind of workaround.

"This is kind of weird, isn't it?" said Nicole. "Why doesn't this hallway have any rooms along it?"

"I always wondered that too, when I was here," said Amy. "I asked one of the court once and he got super weird about it and told me not to worry. In fact, I was transferred out of here soon after that. I almost wonder if that's related."

"There are rooms here, then," said Sister Margaret. "But either the doors are hidden or they're only accessible by stitching."

"And we can't stitch," said Nicole, her voice sharp with frustration.

Sister Margaret shrugged and studied the wall. "But we can cut."

"Without knowing anything about what's behind it?" said Amy. "That seems rash."

"We're behind enemy lines," said Sister Margaret. "We'll need to make some tough decisions."

"Can we at least establish a home base first?" said Nicole. "Amy, how far away are we?"

"It's just around the corner," said Amy. "But let's keep our voices down, right? It's a miracle we haven't come across any–"

Just then, a bland-looking man in a baby blue tuxedo rounded the bend and stopped short, his eyes narrowing at the sight of them. "Agents?" he asked, his voice pinched. "What are you doing in this wing?"

Amy stepped forward. "Hello, Duke Hosner. We're just making our rounds. I'm training these two."

The man's scowl deepened. "Agent Nguyen, isn't it? Are you still assigned to this station?"

"I was just transferred back in last week," she said. "And given the task of training these other new transfers." She took a deep breath. "I was told we're bulking up this station to protect the Pontiff."

That seemed to mollify him. "Well, of course, the Pontiff's safety and comfort must be seen to, and what's left of the high court."

"It's not much, is it?" chimed in Nicole. "Those bastards in St. Louis did a real number on us."

Sister Margaret held her breath. This seemed like a big risk, but the two former agents knew better than she did what the courtier would respond to.

The man's scowl faded and he seemed to relax a little bit more. "Don't worry, agents. The organization will land on its feet. It always does. We'll stamp them down and then the court will be filled anew."

From the gleam in his eye, Sister Margaret figured he had ambitions to advance in the court himself. She wondered if that could be useful. If these lower courtiers could be persuaded to take out more of the higher-ups, that could only help their cause.

Amy cleared her throat. "Let us know if there is anything we can do to help you with that, Duke Hosner."

Sister Margaret wondered if Amy had come to the same conclusion she had.

Duke Hosner studied Amy for a moment and then smiled. "Perhaps there is, at that. An ambitious agent could certainly get on my good side if she was inclined to keep an eye on the prisoner in this wing." He nodded back in the direction they'd come from. "I've heard there was some unrest in one of the other detention wings, and I'd hate for anything to happen to this one."

Sister Margaret suppressed a grin. Jackpot!

"Absolutely!" Amy gushed. "Thank you so much for this opportunity."

Duke Hosner's smile turned smug. "Your cooperation has been noted and will be rewarded."

He continued on his way.

As soon as he disappeared around the next corner, Amy collapsed against the wall. "Holy crap, that was terrifying."

"You pulled it off!" said Nicole, her voice low. "That was fantastic. If I didn't know any better, I'd have one hundred percent thought you were a powergrubber, angling for a working court position."

"He seemed like he bought it too," said Sister Margaret. "And now we know there's a prisoner here."

"And we know there are other detention wings," said Nicole. "Amy? Do you know where the other doorless hallways are?"

"There are five hallways in all without doors," Amy said.

"Are they all detention wings?" asked Sister Margaret. "That seems like a lot, doesn't it?"

"Regular headquarters don't have that many," said Nicole. "They have one wing where all the detainees live, eat, and train."

"I'm pretty sure these ones aren't being trained," said Amy. "I've never heard of anyone coming here to train, have you?"

Nicole shrugged. "I never heard of this place at all until you started talking about it."

"Is this the best spot to be having this discussion?" asked Sister Margaret. "Let's get to our base and then make our plans."

Amy pushed herself off from the wall. "Come on." She led the way around the corner and into a small chamber with three doors. She headed straight to the left one and pushed the door open. "Here we are."

Sister Margaret followed the other two in and immediately sneezed three times. "Well, you're right about it being out of the way."

The room was blanketed in dust.

Nicole frowned. "I'm a little concerned about that duke coming from this direction, though."

Amy waved a hand toward the antechamber. "There's a workroom across the hall that gets a little bit of use. As long as we keep the door to this room shut, it shouldn't be a problem, even if someone comes to use the workroom."

"And the third room?" said Sister Margaret. "What's in there?"

Amy shrugged. "I peeked my head in once. It was as dusty as this room, and full of tattoo equipment. Kind of weird, actually."

"That sounds very weird," said Nicole. "But it sounds like we're probably okay here. So what's the plan?"

"I say we start knocking on the walls," said Sister Margaret. "If anyone answers, maybe we can ascertain whether or not they're one of ours before we let out somebody else."

"Sounds like a good starting place to me," said Amy. "And without being able to use magery to see through the walls, that beats going in completely blind."

Sister Margaret took off her pack, setting it down behind a couch, just in case anyone did come in while they were gone. She wriggled her shoulders, settling her bandolier back into place and readjusting her balance without the backpack.

She ran through a quick weapons check, starting with her serrated boot knives, making sure everything was in its place and easy to unsheath.

Out of the corner of her eye, she saw Nicole and Amy doing the same. They finished, but she was only about halfway through her weapons.

Ignoring her companions' widening eyes, she moved up her body. Needle daggers in the knee sheaths, throwing stars in the flat pockets on the front of her thighs, twin swords at her hips, pepper spray mid-lower-back. That one stuck a little, so she readjusted.

Moving up, she went through all the pockets of her bandolier – cell phone, poison darts, tiny first aid kit, zip ties, vials of spelled potions made by Sister Timothy Ann. Some of those were weapons and some medicinal.

Next her ribcage sheaths with their stiletto knives. One more dagger that lived between her breasts. And finally, she reached over her head and down her back for her bowie knife, grasping the handle and sliding it up just an inch to make sure it was easily accessible.

"All right," she said. "I'm ready."

Amy led the way back down the hallway. She began tapping on the wall as she walked, pausing every few steps to listen for anything from the other side.

Sister Margaret stepped across to the other side, following her lead.

Nicole advanced to the point position, drawing her sword and watching down the hall for any intruders.

The first couple spots Sister Margaret tapped on were definitely hollow, but nobody responded from within.

The third spot sounded solid, like she was tapping into another wall or a stud. She moved down again and tapped a fourth time, listening for any sounds.

"Incoming!" shouted Nicole.

Sister Margaret reacted immediately, drawing her twin swords, but before she could turn and face her opponent, she found herself shoved against the wall, her swords ripped from her hands.

11.

Coyote stitched Trevor and himself out of his bedroom and Trevor blinked in the sudden darkness.

"Coyote?" he called out as his newfound friend's arm left his shoulder where it had rested for the stitch.

"Sorry," said Coyote. Trevor heard a switch flip and blinked as the space filled with light.

He looked around and saw Coyote standing by the door to the small, dusty storeroom.

The room was full of yellowing file boxes, many of them strewn about the floor between the shelves shoved up against the walls. The shelves contained more file boxes.

"I should have warned you it'd be dark," said Coyote. "It's just a nice, convenient spot right next to the detention wing nearest my suite. I figured we'd start here."

"Sounds good," said Trevor. He made his way over to the door, stepping over and around the old boxes.

Coyote opened the door and strode out into the end of a hallway; just an antechamber, really, with three doors and the hallway that continued around the corner.

Trevor followed Coyote into a blank hallway that looked just the same as the one they'd found outside the cell he'd cut Coyote out of.

Coyote marched to the middle of the corridor and, switching his eyes into seer mode, began to slowly pivot, staring at the walls on either side of him.

Trevor focused on switching his own eyes into seer mode, something he had only done a couple of times. It generally didn't come as easily to him as stitching or even spelling.

Nothing happened, so he concentrated harder.

Trevor frowned and poured all of his brainpower into switching on his seer sight.

It still didn't work.

"Is there a problem over there?" asked Coyote. "You look like you're trying to shit out an elephant, and frankly this isn't the time for such things."

Trevor sighed. "I was trying to switch into seer mode, but it isn't working. I mean, seeing isn't my strong suit, but I can usually do it with a little effort."

"Ah." Coyote turned off his own seer sight and moved closer to Trevor. "You're a stitcher, right?"

"Yes."

"Okay." Coyote unsheathed the sword he carried on his back and held it out across his palms. "Stitch this to yourself."

Trevor instinctively moved his fingers in the proper gesture.

Once again, nothing happened.

"Thought so," said Coyote. He resheathed his sword. "It's not just that you're not good at seeing. The bunker is as locked down as it gets. We're going to have to get you doctored up a bit so you can use magery."

Trevor narrowed his eyes. "What does that mean?"

"Got any tattoos?" asked Coyote.

"No," said Trevor.

"That's about to change. Come on." Coyote grabbed Trevor's hand and stitched them into yet another dusty, disused room. "The good news is that now we're right near another detention wing, and I didn't see anyone in the one we were just checking anyway."

Trevor waited for Coyote to turn on the light and looked around. This room was about the same size as the last, but was dominated by a tattoo chair, the kind that was easily adjustable to accommodate its occupant being put into just about any position.

Beside the chair was a metal cabinet, which Coyote bustled over to and opened up.

"Have a seat," said Coyote.

"Absolutely not," said Trevor. "I am not a tattoo person."

"You are if you want to win this fight," said Coyote as he cheerfully pulled a tattoo gun out of the cabinet and brandished it at him.

Trevor scowled and crossed his arms. "Explain, please."

Coyote set down the tattoo gun and lifted up his shirt to reveal a vertical line of tattoos down his side, each about the size of a half dollar, so uniform that they looked like a column of social media logos on a website.

Trevor leaned forward to look at them. "They appear to be alchemical symbols or medieval mage sigils."

"That's right," said Coyote. "Rumor has it the organization has been using these since the very start. You'd be surprised how many people apparently had tattoos in medieval Europe."

"No, I wouldn't," said Trevor as he examined the symbols. "I have a doctorate in medieval history. They would have been brands back then, probably, more than tattoos, but even tattoos were not unheard of."

"Ah. Well. Then if you're still alive after all of this, your field of study will be easy to explain away alchemy symbol tattoos, won't it?" Coyote pointed out.

"I'm not worried about that," said Trevor, straightening up and taking a step back. "I just don't want any tattoos."

"Scared of needles?" guessed Coyote.

Trevor growled. "Maybe a little."

"I've done this before, you know," said Coyote. "I'll be as gentle as a kitten."

"Kittens aren't gentle," Trevor pointed out. "Have you ever had a kitten? They try to climb up your leg like a tree trunk and you end up with scratches galore. To say nothing of those dagger-sharp teeth."

Coyote sighed. "Trevor, the way I see it, you have three options. We can forget about the tattoos and I can stitch you out of the bunker and you can go home without your friend. Or we can forget about the tattoos and try to rescue Tillie and get caught by someone who *can* do magery and all three of us will get killed. Or, and this is the one I like best, I can tattoo these symbols on you with this spelled ink and you'll be able to use magery and we can get your friend and take out some courtiers while we're at it."

Trevor pursed his lips, but finally nodded. "Has anyone ever told you that you have a very persuasive way about you?"

Coyote grinned. "Yes." He turned and pulled a pot of ink out of the cabinet, setting it on top beside the tattoo gun, then turned around to face Trevor again. "Where do you want them?"

"Someplace that doesn't hurt too much and is easy to hide," said Trevor.

"Do you wear shorts a lot?" asked Coyote.

"Almost never," said Trevor.

"Thigh it is. Take those pants off, big boy," said Coyote with a wink. "Time to tat you up."

***

Tillie practiced her krav maga exercises, running through them first empty-handed and then working on ways she could incorporate the tools from the manicure set into her attacks. The jumpsuit she wore had a pocket on the belly, like one of her sister's hoodies, and she had torn strips of bedsheet off, tying them into little pouches and affixing them to the inside of the pocket so she could draw each tool by feel.

The tiny scissors were sharp and could do some real damage, as could the cuticle pusher, if she used them properly.

A small weapon could be just as effective as a large one if applied in just the right spot.

Tillie's lips curved in a small smile.

She might be locked up, but her hair was styled, her nails done, and her makeup perfect. And now she was armed too.

Hearing muffled voices, Tillie spun to face in that direction. The wall was blank except for the number 22 painted on it in orange.

She stepped over to the wall and pressed her ear against it. It sounded like someone was shouting, but she didn't recognize the voice and she couldn't make out any words.

Something large hit the wall, and she jumped back.

Tillie stood, listening, waiting, ready for anything.

***

Sister Margaret struggled to catch her breath as she wrenched her wrists from the grip of her opponent. She hated this feeling – being without her seer sight was a novel experience for her, and she couldn't stand not being able to see what was happening around her and in her near future.

She inhaled deeply and whirled around to face her attacker, kicking out with her left foot.

He turned out to be a guard dressed in the ubiquitous and incredibly impractical orange bikini armor. Grinning at her, he kicked her swords away down the hall before she could bend to scoop either of them up again.

Glancing around, she saw that Nicole and Amy were grappling with another guard each.

Sister Margaret beamed back at the man as he drew a sword of his own and said something in a guttural language – Russian, maybe? If he thought she was helpless without her swords, he was in for a shock.

Ducking his first slash, she threw herself forward, drawing her breast knife as she did so and stabbing upward under his sternum in one smooth motion.

He staggered backward, blood gushing from his wound, and Sister Margaret pulled the knife free, shaking his blood off her hand. She dropped the dagger and reached into her thigh pockets, drawing a throwing star in each hand.

It was trickier to throw them without magesight, but she'd practiced it many times. Silently thanking Sister Catherine for insisting that all of her charges know how to fight without magery, Sister Margaret loosed the star from her right hand toward Nicole's opponent, pivoted, aimed, and threw the other toward the guard Amy was fighting.

"Hey, I had him," Nicole protested. Her enemy was down at her feet, Sister Margaret's star in his throat.

"Well, I didn't," said Amy. "Thanks." The woman she'd been fighting had lurched backward with a star stuck in her belly, but she was still living, her eyes wide as she gasped for breath.

Sister Margaret picked up one of her swords and expertly smacked the guard in the temple, knocking her out.

"Might as well just kill her," Nicole observed. "She'll bleed out before help comes anyway."

Sister Margaret shrugged. "That's in God's hands now. I'll kill in battle. I won't kill someone who can't attack me at the moment."

Nicole nodded. "Any luck with the cells?"

"Not yet," said Sister Margaret. She scanned the wall she'd been checking. "I'm not sure where I left off," she said.

"Right there, I'm guessing," said Amy, pointing to a small red smear on the off-white wall.

Sister Margaret stepped closer to it. It was blood. She frowned. "Is that mine?"

Nicole tapped her forehead and Sister Margaret put a hand up to her own head. Sure enough, it was bleeding.

"Well, would you look at that?" she said. She pulled her first aid kit out of her bandolier and extracted an alcohol wipe and a large square Band-Aid.

Amy held out her hand and Sister Margaret handed them to her, waiting patiently as the stitcher cleaned her small cut and covered it.

"All right," said Sister Margaret. "Shall we get back to it?"

Without waiting for an answer, she stepped back to the wall and began knocking again.

***

Mattie pulled the car into the parking lot of a motel in the middle of nowhere, barely hitting the brake before Chameleon was opening the door and running across the lot to where a small figure was sitting on a bench reading a book.

"That's Elephant?" said Sammy. "Huh."

Mattie turned off the car and watched as the diminutive woman jumped up, dropping her book and barrelling into Chameleon, wrapping her in a big hug.

She slowly opened the car door, reluctant to interrupt their reunion.

Sammy had no such compunctions. He bounced out of the car and strode over to the bench. He picked up the woman's book and studied it, waiting for the two women to finish hugging.

Mattie walked across the parking lot at a more sedate pace. As she approached, Chameleon took a step back. She had tears streaking her face.

Mattie stopped walking, startled.

Elephant broke the tension, dancing in place and giving Sammy and Mattie both a big, sunny smile. "Come on, go ahead," she said. "Get it out of your system."

"You're so small!" said Sammy. "Why are you called Elephant?"

"Elephants have other qualities besides their size," said Elephant. "What else do you know about them?"

"You like to eat peanuts?" Mattie guessed. "You're always squirting water out of your nose?"

Elephant laughed, a raucous giggle. "I like you, honey. You're an asshole, but in a fun way."

"Yeah, I get that a lot," said Mattie with a grin.

"An elephant never forgets?" suggested Sammy.

Elephant made a gun with her fingers and mimed shooting him. "Bingo. I've got an eidetic memory. I'm also kind and have a tendency to go out of my way to rescue people, which elephants do as well."

"Do they?" said Mattie. "That's nice. We are on a rescue mission, so I'm glad to have you on board."

"Getting you literally on board may be a problem, though," said Sammy. He nodded toward the car. "We're pretty full."

Elephant laced her fingers together and stretched her arms out in front of her, cracking her knuckles. "I think we can probably shift things around enough to make it work."

Mattie led the way back to the car, Chameleon and Elephant walking arm-in-arm and Sammy bringing up the rear, carrying Elephant's backpack and book.

The backpack was almost as big as she was, and Mattie found herself wondering how she carried it. And how she'd gotten to this teeny town a half hour drive away from the interstate in the middle of Colorado scrubland.

"Did you hitchhike here?" asked Chameleon, as though she'd read Mattie's mind.

"You know I did," said Elephant. "There are advantages to looking completely and utterly harmless."

"Hah!" Chameleon huffed with laughter. "And how many did you have to disabuse of that notion on this particular trip?"

Elephant giggled again. "Let's see, between New York and here . . . four people were perfectly pleasant. Six men got handsy and were ejected from their cars for their trouble, and two more people got downright murdery."

"What happened to the cars?" asked Sammy.

"What happened to the murderers?" asked Mattie.

"Attempted murderers," Elephant corrected. "I was able to subdue one of them without harm. The other, well, she shouldn't have been trying to dish out what she wasn't willing to take."

"You killed her?" said Sammy, his eyes wide.

"It was her or me," said Elephant with a shrug.

Mattie blinked, but couldn't fault that logic.

"As for the cars," Elephant continued, kicking her left leg forward and shaking it, "With these stubby little legs, it's hard to drive without hand controls or pedal extenders. I can spell them to drive for a while, but eventually it gets tiring, and then of course the previous owners report them stolen, and that's a pain in the ass, so I usually abandon them after a couple hours."

Mattie opened up the trunk and surveyed its contents. If she moved the cooler over a few inches, she could shift that pack over too, and then there should be room for Elephant's backpack.

Moving her fingers, she stitched the items into their spot. It was easier to get things in exactly the right spot using magery than to try to move them by hand. She stitched Elephant's bag into the resulting gap, ignoring Sammy's surprised exclamation as it left his arms.

Now to make room for the new passenger.

Chameleon had already opened up the back door and was pulling things out. A moment later, there was a stack of oblong canvas bags full of weaponry on the pavement.

Mattie studied the trunk, looking back and forth between the meager space available and the bags of swords, knives, and axes.

Finally, she shifted a couple more items and then stitched in two of the three weapons-bags.

"I think that's it," she said, reluctantly. "The other one is going to have to go back in the backseat."

"That's okay," said Elephant. She wiggled her toes, which were exposed in her hiking sandals, the toes painted a bluish gray that made her look sort of corpselike. "I don't need a lot of legroom."

"Fair enough," said Mattie. She carefully shut the trunk with a firm thud.

Elephant easily picked up the heavy weapons-bag in one hand and stowed it on the floor of the back seat behind the passenger seat before climbing in herself.

"I can take a turn at the wheel," Sammy offered, opening the driver's side and leaning against the frame.

Mattie handed him the keys and got into the other side of the back seat.

Chameleon resumed sitting shotgun, and Sammy revved up the engine.

A moment later, they were heading back toward the interstate.

***

The sounds of scuffling only lasted a few minutes, and then Tillie could hear lower voices. She stepped closer to the wall, pressing her ear against it again.

She sighed in frustration. It sounded like at least a couple of people, but all she could hear were muffled murmurs – she couldn't even discern the gender of the speakers.

Suddenly, right beside her head came a rap-rap-rap.

Tillie jumped backward, hand to her chest and stared at the wall for a moment, mind racing.

A moment later, another rap-rap-rap came, a few feet down, but still against the same wall.

This time, Tillie jumped into action. This could be her chance. Either it was someone friendly or something unfriendly, but either way it was a disruption to her status quo and could therefore be a disruption to her imprisonment.

Brandishing the nail scissors in her right hand, she stepped forward again and rapped sharply on the wall with her left.

Immediately, someone shouted on the other side, but she still couldn't make out the damn words.

Tillie turned her fist and pounded on the wall with the side of it.

In response, the person on the other side pounded back.

"Okay, but what is that supposed to mean?" she asked the wall.

Then she jumped back again as the tip of a large blade slid through the wall and began sawing downward.

"Who is out there?" she called.

The blade paused and then disappeared.

A feminine voice said something, but she still couldn't make it out.

"I can't hear you," she shouted as loud as she could.

The knife reappeared and began sawing again with vigor.

Tillie waited, her own weapon raised, although she had to smile at the disparity of the size of the huge serrated blade coming through the wall and the two-inch-long curved manicure scissors she was brandishing.

The knife disappeared after a few inches and then reappeared, moving horizontally this time.

Tillie waited as whoever was on the other side cut a rough square, about four inches on each side. Finally, the last cut intersected with the first one, and the knife disappeared.

She took another step back and another, hoping to be out of range of any weapons that might come through the square hole.

The person on the other side pushed the plaster through, and a familiar face peered through. "*Hola*!" called Sister Margaret with a grin. "You're alive!"

Tillie dropped her nail scissors and began to laugh hysterically. Her knees buckled and she fell to the floor, still laughing

Sister Margaret frowned. "You okay, *chica*? Are you hurt?"

"What's going on?" said Nicole's voice from behind Sister Margaret. "Is it them?"

"Just Tillie, I think, said Sister Margaret. "Help me turn this window into a door." Tillie lay on the floor, her laughter gradually subsiding into hiccups as three knives began frantically sawing into the wall, haphazardly cutting at the top, middle, and bottom.

She pushed herself into a seated position and began carefully sweeping aside pieces of drywall as they were pushed inward, avoiding the knives that frantically continued cutting.

She could hear three voices now, all three beautifully familiar and comforting. Sister Margaret, Nicole, and Amy.

Tillie giggled again, remembering last time she'd been imprisoned in an Auditor cell. It had been Nicole who had rescued her that time too, although to be fair Nicole had also been the one whose orders had put her in there.

Finally, there was a hole in the wall that a person could fit through, and her rescuers pushed their way through in single file.

Amy dropped to her knees beside her, narrowly missing the manicure scissors. "Are you injured?" she asked urgently.

"Only my psyche," said Tillie, giggling. She tapped the side of her head and nodded wisely. "Solitary confinement is not good for your brain, you know."

"I know," said Amy, her brow furrowing. "You were in here by yourself this whole time?"

"Oh, yes and on the train before that," said Tillie. "How long has it been?"

"Nine days," said Nicole. "Do you know where Trevor is?"

Tillie shook her head. "I know he was on the train with me, in the next room. We tapped back and forth. I haven't heard from him since I got here."

"Let's get out of this cell before any more guards come along," said Sister Margaret. "And then we can assess her condition and figure out our next step."

"Her condition," repeated Tillie with another giggle. She shook her finger at the nun. "I'm not pregnant. That's what you say about pregnant women."

"Well, thank goodness you're not, at that," said Sister Margaret. "Let's hope Trevor isn't either."

Nicole and Amy each took one of Tillie's arms as she laughed and Sister Margaret led them out of the cell into a hallway choked with plaster dust.

They guided her past three fallen guards and around a corner.

"Is it far?" she asked. She had managed to stop giggling, but was still having trouble standing. Why was she having so much trouble? She'd been standing just a minute ago and exercising before that. "Am I in shock?" she asked. "I've never been in shock before."

"I think so," said Sister Margaret, turning her head. "We're here, though, and we're going to get some food in you and some water and let you rest for a little while."

"Oh," said Tillie. "That sounds nice."

She allowed Nicole and Amy to lead her to a dusty chair. She sat down and looked around at her surroundings. "Hey, this is that room we saw that one time!"

"Yep," said Amy. "Where we stole the books from. Does it help to see something familiar?"

"You're familiar," said Tillie. She paused. "Burn!"

Amy squinted at her. "What?"

Sister Margaret handed her a bottle of water. "Have you had access to food and water regularly?"

"Oh, yes," said Tillie. "But not a lot of either."

"Don't drink it too fast, then," Sister Margaret cautioned. "What kind of food?"

"Wonderful food," said Tillie. She sipped at the water, careful not to chug even though it tasted fantastic. She knew Sister Margaret was right, and she definitely didn't want to throw up. "Lunch today was crab louie with a delightfully crisp white wine – a viognier, I believe. They don't usually give us wine with lunch, but it was nice. It complimented the salad perfectly. And I had breakfast today too! I don't usually get breakfast, but there was a veggie omelet and a fresh fruit cup. And a mimosa."

"Okay, so if that's actually true, she's probably not too dehydrated," said Nicole. "A salad and fresh fruit are hydrating foods, so even without water, she's probably okay."

"Of course the alcohol would cancel that out at least a little," Amy pointed out.

Tillie sipped the water again. "I'm getting hydrated now," she said. "What's our next step? Do you have any idea where Trevor is?"

Amy shook her head. "We think we know where the other detention areas are, but it's going to be a process of elimination."

"And we're pretty sure the guards know we're here," added Sister Margaret.

"We just hope they don't know exactly where we are," finished Nicole.

Tillie nodded. "Well, sounds like things are good and fucked." She took another sip of water, but choked a little, and water dribbled down her front. She stared down at herself and then looked up at her rescuers. "What are the odds I could get something slightly less completely hideous to wear?"

***

The tattoos didn't hurt as much as Trevor had feared. Coyote assured him that this was because of the location they'd chosen. Apparently his own ribcage ink had hurt like a bitch.

As Coyote started in on tattoo number three, a thought crossed Trevor's mind. "Won't these be sore for a bit while they heal?" he asked. "Maybe we shouldn't have done this if it'll interfere with my fighting abilities."

Coyote shook his head. "You'll be fine. I have some spelled ointment that speeds up the healing process. And honestly, the small amount of discomfort from a fresh tattoo is totally outweighed by the ability to use your mage powers, especially since a fair number of your opponents won't."

Trevor frowned. "Why not? Don't you all have these tattoos?"

"Nope!" Coyote paused to wipe down Trevor's leg, something he seemed to be doing every few minutes. The first couple of times, Trevor was concerned that it would wipe away the tattoo, but apparently that wasn't how it worked. "You now number among the elite. Isn't that nice?"

"Just what I always wanted," said Trevor. "How many more of these are we doing?"

"This is the last one I'm going to give you," said Coyote. "I've got more, but you shouldn't need those. This will give you the ability to do magery in this bunker under the most stringent of lockdowns. Most of the inhabitants can't even use it right now at this level of lockdown."

"Who else can?" asked Trevor.

Coyote didn't answer for a moment, as he drew an intricate curly-lined bit. Finally, he wiped it off and as he moved on said, "The Pontiff, his inner circle of advisors, any other Special agents like me, and guards – the idiots in the orange armor."

"Yeah, why do they wear that ridiculous armor?" asked Trevor. "It protects practically nothing and is impossible to hide."

Coyote shook his head. "Honestly? I don't even know. It's like a holdover from some moronic tradition or other. And that, right there, is the problem with this organization. Well, also it's full of power hungry assholes. But the reason it's absolutely, one hundred percent ready to fall, is that we haven't adapted to this era."

"Do you think the time for secret societies in general is over?" said Trevor. "Or just for this one?"

"It is getting harder and harder to stay undetected in these modern times," said Coyote. "That's undeniable. We've managed to get set up as multiple shell corporations, and it helps that we're international – that muddies the waters a little bit."

"Makes sense."

"But overall, we're still operating on a medieval level. It's absurd," said Coyote. He pointed his ink-stained gloved fingers at Trevor. "Mark my words. This bitch is coming down, and we're going to be the ones who do it. Right here. Right now. You, me, Tillie, Chameleon, probably a few other Specials, the Harpers, the Foxes . . . we can all work together and wipe out the rest of the court, destroy this bunker, and move on with our lives, some of us free to do what we want for the very first time."

Trevor inhaled deeply. "That's powerful stuff, man. I can't say I'm happy to be a part of it – I still kind of wish I'd never gotten involved. But since I am involved, I'm glad I'm fighting by your side."

Coyote grinned. "Me too, brother. Me too."

***

Giovani's eyes fluttered open and he sat up, momentarily disoriented. Why had he been sleeping in his clothes?

He looked around. He was in a motel; nothing odd about that. Where was Agent Ford? The other bed didn't look slept in. He glanced at the clock and jumped to his feet.

5:00? In the evening? Why had he been napping? He never napped.

The last couple of months came flooding back to him.

Agent Ford wasn't there because neither of them were part of the organization anymore. Agent Ford was a Harper, Giovani was a Fox, and they were working to take down the organization, except that he had been a moment behind his team and had gotten locked out of his mission.

He checked his phone and found the message from Mattie telling him to wait. "Fuck."

Giovani had never been good at waiting.

***

Sister Margaret eyed Tillie one last time as she gently closed the door to their base room behind her. She had been sleeping for a couple of hours, and would probably continue to do so for a few more. The poor woman was exhausted from being in high anxiety mode for over a week.

In a perfect world, they would go out now, find Trevor in the next wing they checked, return before Tillie woke up, and get the two of them out of the bunker by morning. They'd reunite with Giovani and start getting things ready for the arrival of the army of Harpers, Warrior Mages, Foxes, and any other mages Sister Catherine could muster up.

And then they'd lay siege to the bunker, smoke out the Pontiff, kill or capture the bastard for real this time, and clean up this secret society once and for all.

Then Sister Margaret could move on to a new mission, which she really hoped would involve all of the stuff the Church was doing right now with the–

Amy, who was in the lead, lifted a hand, derailing Sister Margaret's train of thought.

Sister Margaret loosened her swords in their scabbards, ready to draw if need be, but Amy just pressed herself against the wall, gesturing for Nicole and Sister Margaret to do the same.

Following Amy's lead, Sister Margaret made herself small and silent, waiting for whatever danger she'd spotted to pass by.

After a moment, Amy relaxed and beckoned to her companions to keep following her.

Sister Margaret was used to being in the lead. It was weird having a stitcher lead the way, and one who wasn't even much of a fighter at that. But without the ability to use their mage skills, having a seer take point wasn't of much use, and while Nicole and Sister Margaret were both better warriors, Amy was the only one who really knew the layout of the bunker.

So Sister Margaret swallowed every instinct that told her to take command and followed the stitcher through the labyrinth of hallways.

Finally, the trio reached another doorless hallway and Sister Margaret took charge again. "Same system as before," she ordered. "Amy, you're on that wall. I'll take this one. Nicole, you stand guard." She turned to Amy. "Is this set up the same way as the last one? Where it's a dead end around the corner?"

Amy nodded. "But the rooms around the bend are suites, so we should be more cautious here."

"Who lives there?" asked Sister Margaret.

"I'm not sure anyone does, actually," she said with a shrug. "There aren't a lot of permanent residents here, just like at regular stations. But I know I wasn't allowed in them, and I was told they were private suites."

"I'll do my best to keep that direction in my sights, but I'm going to focus on the other way, as it seems more likely to be the greater danger," said Nicole. She drew her sword and took up position in the center of the hallway, angled so she was mostly facing the most dangerous direction but could still see the dead-end direction peripherally.

Sister Margaret nodded, satisfied, especially as she saw Nicole do a small pivot after a moment.

Turning her attention to the wall, she began knocking lightly, listening, and then moving down to the next section.

Knock-knock-knock. Listen. Move on. Knock-knock-knock. Listen. Move on. Knock-Knock-Knock. Listen. Move on.

Every few feet, she paused to look toward the ends of the hallway, check that Amy was still doing okay, Nicole was still at attention. All was good.

Knock-knock-knock. Listen. Move on. Knock-knock-knock. Listen. Move on. Knock-knock–

"I got something!" cried out Amy. "I hear a voice from inside!"

Sister Margaret rushed to the other wall, pleased to see that Nicole remained on watch.

Pressing her ear to the wall, she heard the muffled voice of a man. "Can you make it out?"

"No," said Amy. "Dammit, I wish we could use magic!"

Nodding, Sister Margaret strained to hear better. She couldn't even tell if it was Trevor's baritone voice or another man. They had no idea how many people were imprisoned here.

"Same thing again," she said, stepping back. "We'll cut a peep hole, see if it's Trevor. If it's not, we'll ask some questions, and then decide if we better spring him or leave him."

She pulled the knife out of her left boot sheath and banged on the wall, hoping that was sufficient warning that the man would move away.

If it was Trevor, he would probably do so. If it was someone who wasn't expecting rescue? Who knew?

She clasped the knife's hilt with both hands and thrust it into the wall, wiggling it up and down a few times before it finally popped through.

Pausing for a moment, Sister Margaret waited to make sure there were no cries of pain coming from the other side.

More muffled yelling came through, but it didn't sound anguished or anything. She pulled the knife back out and examined it for any signs of gore.

All she saw was white dust, so she pushed the knife back in and began sawing, cursing as she did so – this was not her favorite thing to do with a knife.

Her favorite thing to do with a knife was whittle figurines of Saint Joan of Arc, Saint Quiteria, and Saint Martha, all of whom were bad-ass warrior women. Her second favorite thing to do with a knife was whittle figurines of other saints on behalf of her sisters, most of whom wanted boring ones like the Virgin Mary or Francis of Assisi. Her third favorite thing to do with a knife was fight off bad guys.

She wasn't sure exactly where sawing out a square in drywall fit into the list, but it was waaaaay down there.

"Almost done," she muttered as she started on the last side. "Come on, you fucking bastard. Just fucking cut, damn you."

Finally, she got back to the beginning. She pulled the knife back out – almost losing her balance as the blade caught on the ragged edge.

Sister Margaret punched the square, pushing it into the cell, and then waved a hand as dust flew into her eyes. "Fucking hell," she said. "I really hope this is the last fucking time we have to do this."

"Is it him?" asked Amy, behind her.

"Trevor?" Sister Margaret called into the room. "Are you in there?"

"No," said a cold, male voice from inside. "*Trevor* is decidedly not here."

***

Trevor turned his knee inward to get a better look at the three tattoos now gracing his outer thigh. "You do good work," he said. "I'm not going to lie; I was a little afraid they'd look kind of prison-y."

"What do you mean?" asked Coyote as he pulled off his gloves and tossed them into a trash can.

"Oh, you know – like prison tattoos, all unsteady thin lines, drawn on with a pen attached to a sewing needle?" Trevor raised his eyebrows. "You've never seen anything like that?"

"I guess not." Coyote laughed. "You don't strike me as someone who has been to prison. I mean, outside prison. I know you've been in an Auditor cell, and I'm pretty sure it's a very different scenario."

"I have not," said Trevor. "But I know a couple people who have – nothing violent or anything, just drug charges or related stuff. My cousin's got a couple of those prison tats, actually, and she had to get one of them removed because it was on her wrist and she couldn't get a job. Or at least not the jobs she wanted."

"Well, this is not my first rodeo," said Coyote.

Trevor cocked his head. "You're so strange. That just doesn't seem like an idiom someone who has lived his entire life in a secret society would know. But then again, you don't know about things like prison tattoos."

Coyote shrugged. He stood up and began to clean up the tattooing equipment. "I'm not your momma's high courtier – I'm a Special agent. And what's more, I've been undercover in the outside world for much of my life, running a mechanic shop with my dad."

"Your bastard dad?" said Trevor.

Coyote grinned. "Only one I've got."

Trevor went back to studying his new tattoos. "Honestly, I do feel like if I had ever been inclined to get any tattoos, these kind of suit me. These might be ones I would have gotten anyway."

"Glad you like them," said Coyote. He pulled out a small canning jar filled with something thick and bright green and handed it to Trevor. "Slather this on, and don't be coy with it. A good, thick layer. Don't worry about getting it on your clothes; we'll put a bandage over them."

Trevor took the jar. It didn't have a label on it, so he'd just have to trust that Coyote's instructions were correct. Of course, he'd put a lot of trust into Coyote already, so this would be an odd time to stop.

He smiled ruefully and unscrewed the metal lid. A pungent odor smacked him in the nose. "Ughff. Holy shit." Trevor waved his hand over the mouth of the jar, trying – unsuccessfully – to disperse the smell. "I think stealth is off the table if I'm going to smell like this stuff."

Coyote laughed. "It'll be fine. If nothing else, now that you've got the tats, you can spell an olfactory shield over it."

Trevor dipped his fingers in the slimy goo and began to spread it over the fresh ink on his leg, careful not to press too hard on the tender skin. "That sounds like a lot of work," he said. "Maybe once the bandage is over it, that'll suppress the smell."

"That's the spirit," said Coyote. He leaned over to assess Trevor's work. "More. Really slather it on. Like you're frosting a cake, not like you're putting on sunscreen."

Trevor wrinkled his nose, but scooped out another huge dollop and glomped it on.

"That's it," said Coyote. He laid out a roll of tape and a few paper-wrapped square bandages, ready for Trevor to finish.

Trevor spread out the ointment and looked at Coyote for approval.

Coyote lifted his eyebrows, and Trevor sighed and pulled out another scoop of the foul stuff. At this point, he was almost at half the jar. He spread it on and mimicked Coyote's facial expression.

Laughing, Coyote raised his hands in surrender. "Okay, that's enough. But we'll take the rest with us to reapply as needed."

Trevor couldn't get the lid back on the ointment fast enough. As Coyote covered it all up with the bandages, Trevor leaned over to snag a towel from the cabinet, wiping his hands clean.

Finally, Coyote put the final strip of tape on and stood up. "All right. We're good to go."

***

"Who are you?" Sister Margaret demanded. "Why did they put you in this cell?"

"No, no, no," said the man. "I will ask the questions here. I don't recognize your voice, agent. When were you assigned to this bunker?"

A face appeared in the hole as the man peered out at them.

Amy's face paled and she took a step backward, grabbing Sister Margaret's arm and dragging her back with her.

The man's face lit up. "Agent Nguyen! You, I know."

"Stay back," Amy hissed. "Don't let him reach you."

Sister Margaret narrowed her eyes and studied the man's cruel face. He was not handsome, but something about him oozed charisma nevertheless. He had a large, hawklike nose and the kind of eyebrows that seemed designed to lift into sardonic hooks. Across the middle of his face, a dark handlebar mustache gleamed, the tips waxed upward.

"And I know that you're no longer with the organization," he said sadly. His eyes widened deliberately as though to show contrition. "I was so sad to hear that."

"The fuck you were," said Amy.

"Okay, so obviously we're not letting this guy out," said Nicole. "What do we do about the hole?"

The man rolled his eyes. "Oh, no! You're not going to let me out? Whatever shall I do?"

"You'll stay the fuck put," said Sister Margaret. "And work on your mustache some more."

"Will I?" the man pretended to consider this. And then shook his head. "I don't think I will, actually."

He moved his face back and reached his arm out through the hole. As soon as his hand and wrist were out, he made a stitching motion. "Ah," he said. "I see how it is. You people must be causing some trouble out here, if even the hallways are no magic zones."

"We're doing our best," said Sister Margaret.

"No matter," he said. He reached his arm out further, straining to get the entire arm through the small square.

Sister Margaret shifted her grip on the hunting knife as she and Amy backed up further to make sure they were out of his reach. She wasn't afraid to use the knife, of course, but contrary to popular belief, she did prefer to avoid violence wherever possible.

The creep acknowledged the move with a smug twist of his lips, but made no effort to reach for them. Instead, he braced his hand against the wall and pressed himself against the wall as though he was trying to fit his entire body out through the hole.

Which was ridiculous. He wouldn't even be able to fit his head through it.

Finally, his entire arm was out in the hallway, up to the shoulder.

"You see," he said, his voice strained with effort. "No one can use magery in the cell, no matter who they are. But out here –" he wiggled his arm "–someone like me can."

"Oh, no!" said Amy. She jumped forward and grabbed his wrist, grappling with it. "Get his arm back in! He must have keyed tattoos on it!"

Suddenly it all made sense. Sister Margaret herself had spelled tattoos that responded to security spells in the convent she had sworn to defend.

The man swung his arm and Amy staggered back against the far wall, clutching her face where he had smacked her.

Leaping forward, Sister Margaret slashed toward the man's arm, hoping he would instinctively retreat.

Instead, he called her bluff and her knife swished against the sleeve of his jumpsuit.

Before she could slash again – and this time she wouldn't be bluffing; these hunting knives could cut through bone with no problem – he laughed, made his stitching gesture again, and disappeared.

***

Mattie slammed on the brake as a person appeared in the middle of her lane directly in front of the car. The car began to skid, and she realized that at highway speed, slamming on the brakes wasn't a good idea.

"Fuck, fuck, fuck, fuck, fuck!" she yelled as she lifted her foot off the brake and swerved into the other lane, narrowly missing the rear bumper of a black van that had just passed her.

The van honked loudly and sped up, leaving her in its dust. Nobody else was behind her, so Mattie slowly pulled back into the right lane and then onto the shoulder, finally rolling to a stop, her eyes wide and her hands shaking.

The car was barely stopped when Chameleon and Elephant flung their doors open, jumping out and running back toward the figure, who was still standing in the same spot they'd stitched into.

In the rearview mirror, Mattoe could see the newcomer lift their hands, which began to glow.

Mattie hastily flung up a shield between the car and the figure.

"What the fuck is happening right now?" Sammy demanded. He had clearly been asleep again – other than the brief driving stint he had taken after picking up Elephant, Sammy had spent the entire trip napping in the back seat.

"I don't know," said Mattie, grimly. "But I don't think that's a friend of theirs."

Her shaking subsided and she opened her car door, heading for the action, which had thankfully moved off the freeway and into the ditch beside it.

They were far from any cities and the highway wasn't busy, but it wasn't deserted either.

Mattie ran toward the three mages, who were evenly spread out in a triangle, facing off. Chameleon and Elephant had their backs to her.

She slowed to a walk as she got about 500 feet from the stand-off, turning on her mage sight.

Action may have been a strong word to describe what was happening in front of her.

Even in the future, her mage sight showed no spells flying; the three of them were just standing there staring at each other.

Relaxing slightly, Mattie stopped walking and studied the new mage. Even up close, she still couldn't tell if they were a man or a woman. Their loose, androgynous clothing and short buzzed hair style had her wondering if maybe they identified as nonbinary.

She couldn't really tell their age either – they had a smooth, unlined face that implied youth, but something about them seemed more mature. She couldn't quite put her finger on why.

Whoever they were, she was tired of waiting to see what was going to happen.

"Hey!" she called out. "What the fuck is going on?"

"Get back in the car," said Chameleon without turning around. "This is between Specials. It doesn't concern you."

Mattie crossed her arms. "Does that really seem like something I would do?" she asked.

None of the three moved or responded for a good thirty seconds. Mattie waited.

"No," said Chameleon finally. "But it's something I'd like you to do."

"Tough titties," she said. "I've got your back. Is this a fight, though, or is it a staring contest or something else entirely?"

"Kind of looks like a coven meeting from a movie," said Sammy from right behind her.

Mattie whirled around. "You are like a damn ninja," she gasped. "Have you been behind me this whole time?"

He shrugged. "Yeah. I followed you from the car."

Mattie forced her breathing into a steadier rhythm. Feeling calmer, she turned back around and narrowed her eyes. Had the three of them moved closer together?

"Are they moving?" asked Sammy in a low voice. "I think they're moving, but like really, really slowly."

Mattie fixed her eyes on Chameleon and realized she was floating a couple inches off the ground and was, in fact, steadily advancing.

Elephant was doing the same.

The new mage was too far away for Mattie to see if they were following suit.

"This is so weird." Sammy's comment echoed Mattie's thoughts. "I can't even tell if they're enemies or . . . ?"

"I think enemies," said Mattie. "I mean, why would a friend stitch into the middle of the road and almost make us crash?"

"They're pretty confident, too, assuming we wouldn't just run them over," said Sammy.

"I wonder if they were expecting one of the Specials to be driving," said Mattie. "Maybe it threw a wrench in their plans when it turned out to be me."

"Honestly, I'm just so glad we switched at the last stop," said Sammy. "I'm pretty sure I would have just run them over."

"I almost did too," said Mattie. "Wait. Something's happening."

She jogged a few steps forward to catch up with the triangle of Specials. The whole formation had definitely moved, newcomer and all. It did look a little smaller, but not by a lot.

Suddenly, based on no signal she saw, everything exploded into a full-blown mage battle, with fireballs and lightning flying.

"Fuck!" screamed Sammy. He fell to the ground beside her, and Mattie threw up a mage shield and then knelt down.

"Are you hit?" she asked. "What happened?"

The sleeve of his t-shirt was smoldering, and she grabbed it and ripped it free from the rest of the shirt.

"I think I'm okay," said Sammy through gritted teeth. "The shirt got the brunt of it. That was my favorite shirt, though."

Mattie raised an eyebrow. "That shirt? That was your favorite shirt?"

It was a neon yellow and read *Sorry, girls. I'm gay!* in rainbow letters.

"What? It's awesome," he said. "And not everyone can pull off this color, you know."

"Well, that's true," she said. He did actually look fabulous in that color. "But nobody thinks you're anything but gay after talking to you for literally thirty seconds. The shirt is superfluous."

Sammy put a hand to his chest and smiled modestly. "Thank you. You don't know what that means to me."

Mattie rolled her eyes. "Okay, well, you seem unhurt. Are you unhurt?"

"Yeah," said Sammy. He craned his neck to look at his arm. "I don't think I'm even burnt. I was just startled."

"Great." Mattie helped him to his feet and turned back toward the three Specials.

Who were now hugging.

"I am so confused," said Sammy. "Also, and I'm just gonna say this now, if whoever that is thinks they're riding with us, I am so not sitting bitch."

***

Giovani tossed back the shot of whiskey in front of him and grimaced with instant regret. Maybe whiskey wasn't really what he needed right now. He definitely needed some kind of booze, though, and he knew better than to switch up after he'd already started.

He beckoned to the aging platinum diva who was tending bar.

She smiled at him. "Rough day, hon? Get you another?"

"Not the well again," he said. "How about a Jameson on the rocks? Double."

"You got it." She half-turned and pulled a green bottle from the row of liquors behind her, setting it down on the bar. Reaching for a glass, she eyed Giovani. "Weren't you in here with a group the other night? What happened to your friends?"

"They're busy tonight," he said. "I'm on my own for the evening."

"Is that so?" The bartender crossed her arms to better display her cleavage and leaned forward on the bar. "Good-looking guy like you don't ever need to be on his own."

Giovani smiled tightly. "Just the Jameson, please," he said.

Unconcerned, the blonde straightened up and scooped ice into the glass, following it up with the Irish whiskey. "Let me know if you wanna put in a food order. Kitchen closes at midnight."

Giovani glanced at the clock above the bar mirror. "It's only eight."

She set the drink down in front of him. "You look like you're gonna be here a while. Six bucks."

He opened his wallet and pulled out a ten. "You're very astute, ma'am. Keep the change."

She smirked at him, tucked the bill into her bra, and ambled off toward a group of young men at the other end of the bar.

Giovani sipped his drink. A much more enjoyable libation, and one less likely to end in vomit.

As he savored the rich sweetness of the whiskey, Giovani turned his attention to Sister Margaret's tablet, which she had left behind in the room, and which he had brought with him to the bar to go over the notes taken during the period of scrying they'd undertaken.

He unlocked the screen using Sister Margaret's numeric code and opened up the notes app. As he was about to tap the top entry, his attention was caught by the next one down.

"Broken Bunker layout?" he murmured. "Well, that sounds helpful."

He tapped on it and found a series of flowcharts of wings, hallways, and rooms. Attached to several of the entries were notes like, *Amy thinks this was empty* or *Not allowed down that hall.*

Giovani studied the charts, but found himself getting confused. This format didn't really make sense for his brain.

He looked up, but the bartender was nowhere to be found. Glancing around the room, he saw her clearing a table near the back.

He waited patiently, watching her as she finished that table and then disappeared into the kitchen. She emerged a minute later with a tray full of plates and delivered them to another table, laughing and chatting with the group seated there, and then she finally bustled back to the bar.

"Excuse me, ma'am?" Giovani called down to her as she stopped in front of her cash register.

"Sassy," she called back.

Giovani blinked. "Excuse me?" he repeated.

"Folks around here call me Sassy," she said. She finished up whatever she was doing with the register and ambled over to him. "You want to see a menu?"

"No, no," he said, still distracted by the notion that 'Sassy' was a name. "Um. I was just wondering if you might have some paper and a pencil I could use."

"Sure, hon. What kind of paper?"

"Uh. Regular?"

She raised her eyebrows and pulled a small notebook out of her apron pocket. "You want something like this? Or something bigger?"

"Oh. Bigger, please," he said.

"Lines?"

"No. Yes. Dealer's choice." Giovani shrugged. "Sorry."

"All good, hon. I'll grab you something from the office." Sassy sashayed back into the kitchen, appearing a minute later with a small stack of multi-colored printer paper. She set it down in front of Giovani. "Will this work? It's got fliers on one side, but you can doodle on the back."

"That's perfect." He looked around. "And a pencil?"

"Oh, sure." Sassy felt around on the back of her head, finally pulling a pencil out of her messy bun. It must have been load bearing, because a few strands of hair fell down around her face as it emerged.

"Thanks." Giovani took the pencil gingerly.

"It's not gonna bite, just because it was in my hair," said Sassy with a laugh. "I wash it regular."

"Sorry. Of course." Giovani clutched the pencil more firmly. "Thanks again."

"You bet your bonnet, hon." Sassy smiled and ambled away again to lean on her forearms against the bar a few feet down, surveying her small kingdom.

Giovani pulled the top sheet off the stack of papers, consulted the first of the flowcharts, and began to draw out a map.

**

Trevor followed Coyote out the door of the tattoo studio and into a short hallway with two other doors off of it. "This is the prison wing?" he said.

"Just around the bend," said Coyote. He led the way to the corner, but stopped short as soon as he turned. "Huh."

"What's going—" Trevor peered around Coyote. "Oh."

This hallway had no *official* doors off it, but just a couple feet in was a dusty pile of irregular chunks of drywall in front of a rough hole in the wall.

"Is this the cell I broke you out of?" asked Trevor.

"No, I don't believe it is," said Coyote. "We cut a pretty neat rectangle in that wall."

"This one looks more like something the Kool-Aid guy broke through," Trevor observed. He walked around Coyote and down the hall to take a closer look.

"Which means either someone fucked with our hole after we cut it or someone else is going around cutting people out of prison cells and isn't as fastidious about it," said Coyote. "Easy enough to find out." He stepped into the cell and turned around. "Different cell number," he called through the hole. "This is absolutely the work of someone else."

"Lewis said there were four of us," Trevor said. "That's me, you, Tillie, and someone else." He followed Coyote into the cell.

"So, was this Tillie's cell or someone else's?" Coyote asked.

Trevor squatted and picked up a pair of nail scissors from the floor and studied them. "How can we know?"

Coyote nodded at the scissors. "Is your girl into manicures?"

Trevor shrugged. "She's not my girl, but yes."

"Then again, so are a lot of people," said Coyote. "This would be easier if we knew who the other person was. Lewis didn't give you any information on that count?"

"I don't think he knew," said Trevor. "Doyle certainly didn't. She didn't want me to release anybody except Tillie. Said they would probably be court and would just turn on me."

"She's not wrong," said Coyote, absently. "And anyone from the court is also likely to be doing their nails. Or holding onto the scissors in case they can be used as a weapon."

"Why would they leave weapons so readily available?" asked Trevor.

"Hubris," said Coyote. He wandered over to the bed and pulled back the comforter. "Bed's made. Would Tillie have made her bed?"

"Yes," said Trevor. He spotted something on the pillow and strode over to pick it up. Holding up a four-inch-long strand of auburn hair, he grinned. "And she also has red hair."

"Well done, Trevor!" said Coyote. "I feel like I should have caught that."

Trevor shrugged. "You would have. So, this means Tillie is probably free, right?"

"Red hair isn't super common," said Coyote. "Although there are a surprising number of redheaded characters in fiction. Like disproportionately a lot."

Trevor eyed his companion. "So?"

"So, why are redheads so fascinating to authors?" said Coyote. "It's kind of weird."

"Okay," said Trevor.

Coyote shrugged. "Never mind. The point is that it's not impossible that both our courtier and Tillie have red hair, but it's statistically unlikely. So, yes, Tillie is probably free. Somehow."

"Great," said Trevor.

"Not really," said Coyote. "Up until now, there were only a couple of places we needed to check to find her. Now she could be anywhere in the bunker."

"How big can a bunker be?" asked Trevor.

Coyote stared at him. "Have you ever known the organization to do anything half-assed?"

"No," Trevor admitted.

"This bunker is roughly the size of Central Park."

"That's over a mile of area," said Trevor.

"Yes," said Coyote, moving toward the hole in the wall. "It is."

"Oh," said Trevor. "Well, fuck."

***

Tillie woke up midair, arms flailing as she fell off the couch she'd been sleeping on, and landed with a bruising thud on her backside. "Oh," she groaned. "Crap."

Rolling over, she pushed herself up to her hands and knees and then leveraged her body upright using the narrow sofa she had inhabited so recently. She eyed the offending piece of furniture and gave the leg a halfhearted kick.

With a sigh, she looked around the room she was in. "All alone again," she said. "This sucks."

Tillie swiveled, searching for any clues as to where her friends had gone, and spied a piece of paper sitting on an end table. "I suppose I should be glad there wasn't a coffee table in front of that couch with sharp corners," she muttered as she picked up the note and unfolded it. "'Gone to rescue Trevor. Back soon,'" she read aloud. "'There's food in the backpacks.'"

Sitting down, she rummaged through one of the packs, finding jerky and water. "At least the Auditors fed me proper food."

Even so, she felt her mood rising as she munched on the tough meat. Sure, anyone would be grumpy to wake up alone, falling off a couch. But she was free!

Tillie experimentally shifted her eyes, trying to move into seer mode. No dice. She sighed.

"Well, I'm in a library anyway," she said. She stood up and wandered over to a bookcase to browse. "But we already took all the good books out of here, didn't we?"

Then she spotted a shape in the corner of the room, something large covered in a grubby white sheet. "Is that ... ?"

Pulling the cover from the object, Tillie smiled widely. "That's more like it."

She drew the bench back from the baby grand piano to sit down and reverently lifted the cover from the keys. "I don't suppose it's in tune, but ..."

Tillie settled her fingers in place and began to play her favorite Beethoven sonata. Pausing to mutter the words to a sound shield, Tillie settled her fingers in place and began to play her favorite Beethoven sonata, so intent on her task that she didn't notice that her fingers weren't glowing, and no shield snapped into place.

To her astonishment, the sound was sweet and perfectly well-pitched. She smiled, pure pleasure filling her soul. "It must be magic," she murmured.

Closing her eyes, Tillie lost herself in the music.

12.

As Mattie helped Sammy to his feet, the trio of other mages walked toward them, arm in arm.

"I guess they're friends now," said Sammy. "Do you know who the other person is?"

"No idea," said Mattie. "Gotta be another Special agent, right?"

"With some kind of animal name," said Sammy. "What do you think it is?"

Mattie tried to remember the list that she and Chameleon had discussed, but all the names sort of ran together after a while. "Rattlesnake," she guessed. "They could be a Rattlesnake."

"I'm gonna go with Komodo Dragon," said Sammy.

"Why?" asked Mattie.

"First animal that pops into my mind when I look at them."

She tried to remember if there was a Komodo Dragon on the roster. "I don't think that's one of them."

The group was moving slowly and she could see the newcomer, who was in the middle, was limping slightly. Mattie wondered why they didn't just levitate.

Finally, they stopped a few feet away.

"So, what's the story here?" asked Sammy. "Are we taking this one along too?"

"I have my own vehicle," said the new mage.

Mattie was startled by the high, girlish timbre of the voice.

"Hi," said Sammy, stepping forward and holding out his hand. "I'm Sammy."

The mage looked at his hand and then up at his face and back to his hand. Finally, they freed their right arm from Elephant's and tentatively reached for Sammy's hand. "Raccoon."

Mattie's eyebrows shot up and she took an involuntary step backward.

Raccoon fixed her bright blue eyes on Mattie's face and the corner of her mouth quirked upward. "I see you've heard of me."

Chameleon marched to the open driver's door of the Corolla and leaned against it. "No more time to waste," she said.

Suddenly she was in a hurry? Mattie blinked at her.

"Raccoon, you'll take Elephant with you. We'll all be more comfortable spread out a little."

Raccoon nodded, took Elephant's arm again, and stitched out.

Mattie walked toward the passenger's side of the car. "So, we trust her now?"

"Of course," said Chameleon. "You saw what happened."

"Did I?" Mattie slid into the seat and slammed the door more forcefully than she meant to. She was so tired of feeling like she was just one step behind at all times.

"Sure," said Chameleon, starting the engine. "You were right there."

"Were we?" said Sammy from the back seat.

"Raccoon is on our side," said Chameleon firmly. "She and Elephant will gather the others. We will make haste to the bunker."

"What others?" asked Sammy.

"The others," said Chameleon. As she pulled onto the freeway she began listing them off. "Meerkat, Bonobo, Rattlesnake, Coyote."

"I thought Coyote was already inside," said Mattie.

"Yes, that's right," said Chameleon. "I forgot. We'll rendezvous with Coyote once we arrive."

"When will we arrive?" asked Sammy.

Mattie grabbed her phone and typed the name of the town into the GPS, setting the starting point as the current location. "Four hours." She glanced at the clock. "We'll get there around midnight."

Chameleon pushed down on the gas pedal. "We'll be there before that."

Mattie noticed she had a couple of texts and a missed call from Sister Catherine, but before she could click through, the phone went dark. "Shit!"

Rummaging in her purse, she realized she hadn't packed a charger. She turned around to peer back at Sammy. "Hey, what kind of phone do you have?"

He held his phone up for her to see, and she squinted at the charging port. It didn't match.

No point in asking Chameleon – there was no way her old flip phone would have the same charging style.

She would just have to go without. She hoped the communiques she'd missed weren't super important.

***

Trevor had to stoop slightly to get back out of the cell through the ragged hole in the wall. Out in the hallway, he turned to head further down, but stopped. "Do you hear that?" he asked.

Coyote was dusting himself off, a grimace of distaste on his face. "Third time today I'm covered in this shit, and I have to say, it's not my favorite."

"Shh!" Trevor pivoted, walking back the way they'd come. "I know that song."

"I think you usually refer to classical music as a 'piece,' not a song," Coyote observed, but he followed Trevor toward the dead end alcove.

"It's Beethoven," Trevor said softly. "It's Tillie's favorite. She plays it all the time."

He pressed his ear to the first door on his left, right across from the room he'd spent the past few hours being tattooed in. Was she really this close the whole time?

Trevor reached for the knob, but his hand was shaking and he couldn't open it. What if it wasn't her? He wasn't sure he could stand it.

"I just keep losing her," he murmured. He met Coyote's puzzled eyes and tried to explain. "We've been joined at the hip since we were children. We grew up on the same street, went to the same school. After that, I went to college and she got married. It didn't last, and after her divorce, we moved into this teeny little apartment together. She went to massage school, graduated, started massaging, and then realized she could make more if she offered . . . other services. Around the same time, I was in grad school and was figuring my own self out; realizing why I had never been able to make any romantic relationships work, and why I didn't even really want to and had only tried to because of, you know, society. We both realized we didn't give a shit about what society wanted, and we were going to do our own thing, but we were doing it together." He leaned against the wall beside the door. "I thought we shared everything. I certainly shared everything with her."

He went silent as he felt a tear slide from his eyes. After a moment, he cleared his throat and continued. "I only found out otherwise a couple of months ago. She disappeared, ran off, away from the Auditors. I went looking for her and found . . . all of this." Trevor waved his hand to encompass the bunker, the organization, and magery in general. "And I found her again. But things have been strained between us. How could they not be? She hid this massive part of her life from me. But I still love her so much."

The tears were flowing freely now, and Coyote handed him a soft folded square of cloth.

Trevor wiped his cheeks and his eyes with the handkerchief and shook his head, pulling himself together. "And then we argued. Right before we were kidnapped, we got into this ridiculous fight. It was just stress and nerves and the build-up of words that should have been said before but weren't."

"That'll happen," said Coyote. He nodded toward the door. "It would probably help you to tell her all of this."

Trevor nodded. Music still flowed from within, but it had shifted to a Schubert piece. Trevor smiled. "This one is my favorite."

"Well, that's an opening if I ever heard one!" said Coyote. He put his hand on the doorknob and raised his eyebrows in question.

Trevor lifted his chin, squared his shoulders, and nodded. "Let's go."

In perfect dramatic fashion, Coyote opened the door just as the music crescendoed.

Striding into the library, Trevor went straight to the piano, sat down beside Tillie and set his fingers on the keys. He closed his eyes and waited for the perfect moment.

And then he began to play.

The music rose, their duet dancing together perfectly, just as they'd done so many times before. It felt like nothing had changed, and Trevor found his eyes welling up again, the tears leaking out through his still-closed eyelids.

The piece ended, and he sat perfectly still for a moment, waiting, although he couldn't have told anyone what he was hoping for.

After a moment, a head leaned against his shoulder at exactly the spot Tillie's head always landed. Without thinking, Trevor slid his arm around her shoulders in just the way he always did.

And just for that moment, all was right in the world.

***

Giovani's pencil flew across the paper, his mind somehow translating the flowcharts into a map without pause. He reached for another sheet of paper, fitting it against the first one, and filled that one too.

It felt like only a few minutes later when he set down the pencil, lifted his head, and picked up his drink again.

He frowned at the glass. What had happened to the ice?

Glancing up at the clock, his eyes widened. He'd been working for two and a half hours?

Giovani surveyed the spread of the pages on the bar in front of him. The map encompassed four sheets – three that ran in a row and one lower one that branched off from the middle. He picked up the central page, which had several odd blank portions, and looked from the map to the chart on the tablet.

Clearly, there were entire areas of the bunker that Amy simply hadn't been allowed to familiarize herself with. "Those are the parts to pay attention to," he muttered.

As he set the page down, carefully lining it back up with the pages that bracketed it, his stomach rumbled.

Looking around, he saw Sassy heading toward him, and he lifted a hand to get her attention.

Sassy smiled broadly at him and hastened her pace, arriving behind the bar in a moment. "Well, well," she said. "He emerges! Do you know, I tried to ask you three times if you needed anything, and you were just zoned in."

"Oh, sorry," he said. "I do that sometimes."

"No, you're good. Must be nice to be able to focus like that." She leaned against her arms on the bar. "What are you working on, anyway?"

"Uh, just a project. For work," he hedged.

"What do you do, hon?" she asked.

Giovani's mind went completely blank. "That's classified," he blurted out.

He froze. Of all the things to say. . . . Suddenly, he could think of a million different careers that would have been perfectly reasonable – architect, cartographer, surveyor. So many reasons to be making a map.

But no. He had said, *That's classified.*

Sassy just laughed. "Okay, okay. Keep your man of mystery aura. No skin off my nose."

"Could I see a food menu?" he mumbled, running a hand over his hair.

"Sure thing, hon." Sassy reached behind her and grabbed a laminated trifold menu. "Take your time." She nodded toward someone behind him and ambled off in that direction.

"That's classified," Giovani muttered to himself again. "Of all the idiotic . . . oh, spinach dip sounds good."

The menu was comprehensive and ran the gamut from burgers and fries to pad thai and spring rolls.

That would have surprised a lot of people, but Giovani had spent a lot of time in small towns like this. He knew that in a place with only two or three eateries, bars and restaurants tended to cover all the bases to serve as many tastes as possible.

Sassy sauntered back. "Have we decided?"

"Yeah," he said. "I will have the spinach dip to start and a mushroom swiss burger."

"Fries with that?"

"No, thank you. And another Jameson."

"You got it." Sassy held out her hand, and Giovani gave her back the menu.

As she left to enter in his order, he slung back the watered down whiskey. No sense in wasting it. He set down the glass and glanced at the stern-looking man who had just come up to lean against the bar right next to him.

Why did people do that? There were acres of unpopulated bar further down, but this guy had to stand right next to the only person seated there. He would have been better served just a couple feet down, where Sassy was standing at the register.

Giovani grimaced and began to gather up the pages of his map before anything could spill on them.

"What's that?" asked the man, craning his head to look at his work.

Giovani smiled tightly and casually folded them up so the man wouldn't be able to get a good look. He probably wouldn't know what he was looking at, but you couldn't be too careful. "Just a rough mock-up," he said.

"Of what?" The man's eyes were piercing, and Giovani was now not so sure that he wasn't an Auditor spy.

"I'm an architect," said Giovani. "It's just a project I'm working on."

"Let me see." A cold, viselike hand gripped Giovani's wrist.

Giovani's hands pulsed with a brief glow as he sent a tiny spark of lightning backward from his hand toward the other man's. He met the man's chilly gray eyes, which seemed somehow out of place on his face, prompting Giovani to wonder for a split second if the man was wearing colored contact lenses.

Then Sassy slammed her palm down on the bar, startling both men.

The stranger released Giovani's hand, and Giovani snatched it back, gathering up the map and the tablet quickly and shoving them into his backpack.

"Are you drunk, Gonzalez?" Sassy demanded. "What do you think you're doing, placing hands on my customers?"

Gonzalez raised both hands in surrender. "My apologies, Sarah. I thought I saw something strange in this gentleman's papers, but I must have been mistaken."

Sassy rolled her eyes. "How many times do I have to ask you not to call me Sarah."

"But that is your name," said Gonzalez.

"And nobody but my grandma uses it," said Sassy. "Now, you know the drill." She pointed to a line of electrical tape laid out on the floor. "Walk the line. If you can do it, you can have another drink. If you can't, you walk home now."

"That won't be necessary," said Gonzalez. "I am done for the evening." He pivoted on his heel and made a beeline for the front door.

Sassy shook her head and eyed Giovani. "You all right, hon? Mr. Gonzalez is an odd duck, but I don't think he means any harm."

Giovani nodded. "I'd like to settle up my bill now," he said, abruptly.

"Oh, sure." Sassy reached into her apron and consulted her notepad, tearing off a page and slapping it down on the bar in front of him. "It's gonna be $21."

Giovani handed her a twenty and six ones. "How long until the food will be out?"

"Oh, your dip'll just be a few minutes. The burger, probably about ten."

"Would you mind holding them for me?" he asked, dismounting from his bar stool.

"Sure, hon. Going out for a smoke?"

"Something like that." Giovani slung his backpack over one shoulder and followed the same path as Gonzalez toward the door. He pushed it open and stepped out into the muggy summer night. After the air conditioned bar, it felt heavy and oppressive, even this late into the evening.

As he'd suspected, Gonzalez was still outside. He sat on a bench overlooking the parking lot, smoking a cigarette.

Giovani wrinkled his nose but approached, stopping about ten feet away. He waited. It was almost always better to let the other person talk first, unless you had the element of surprise on your side.

"What's your name?" asked Gonzalez finally. He didn't turn his head, but kept staring out into the parking lot and beyond to the brightly lit service station across the way.

"Giovani." He didn't see any reason to lie, but he also wasn't going to volunteer anything extra.

Gonzalez nodded. "First name."

It didn't sound like a question, so Giovani didn't respond, just stood and waited for whatever would come next.

Gonzalez let out a stream of smoke. "Speller?"

"Morpher," said Giovani. He'd be able to tell a lot about the man by his reaction to that term.

"Hm." Gonzalez grunted and took another drag off his cigarette.

Giovani thought about that for a moment. Gonzalez wasn't confused by the term, which argued for some familiarity with the Auditor court. He wasn't shocked and angry about it, so he probably wasn't an agent or at least not a loyal one. He was dressed in blue jeans and a flannel shirt, so if he was a Harper, he was careful not to advertise it – their uniform was a black suit. Was there another organization he wasn't familiar with?

Or was Gonzalez something else altogether?

On a hunch, Giovani finally asked a question himself. "Do you know a woman named Chameleon?"

"That's an odd name for a woman," said Gonzalez.

"No odder than Sassy," said Giovani.

"It's a great deal odder than Sassy, actually," said Gonzalez. "It's downright peculiar."

"Ah." Giovani turned around to go back into the bar.

"I know a woman named Madeleine," said Gonzalez.

Giovani stopped and eyed Gonzalez sideways. He waited, but Gonzalez didn't say anything more, just stubbed out his cigarette, tossed the butt into the bucket of sand that sat next to the bench, and stood up.

His boot heels clicked ponderously on the pavement as he walked across the parking lot and disappeared into the night.

Giovani went back into the bar and ate his meal.

13.

Sister Margaret reached the end of the hallway and turned around to lean against the wall. Her bowie knife dug into her back, but she didn't bother adjusting it. She was used to various weaponry being vaguely uncomfortable – as long as nothing interfered with movement, she'd learned to ignore the discomfort.

"Nothing over here," said Amy, facing her from across the hall.

"What next?" asked Nicole. Her voice was dull and heavy.

Sister Margaret shook her head. "We're all exhausted. It's been a long day, and if we don't get some rest, we won't be able to defend ourselves, even against the likes of these." She kicked her foot out toward the pile of bodies that lay behind down the hall from them, the remnants of another group of guards who had stumbled across them in their hunt for Trevor and been dispatched.

The only advantage the guards had over her and her friends was that they were still able to use magery. They were terrible fighters, poorly armed, and their armor was laughable. It felt almost unsportsmanlike to kill them, but if someone was trying to kill her, that's what she was going to do, every time.

They had also run into a lot of agents throughout the day, and she felt even more guilty about killing them. Most of the agents had been better fighters than the guards, but hadn't been using magery. And it was clear that they hadn't practiced fighting without magery the way she had.

Then there had been the courtiers, most of whom were terrible fighters *and* lacked magery.

Sister Margaret had been surprised by the sheer number of people they'd had to fight off – this bunker must be enormous to host so many.

Amy had been surprised too; there hadn't been so many occupants when she'd been stationed at the bunker.

The organization must have known the fight was coming here, and sent everyone it had left. Either that or they had simply sent everyone to their most fortified location.

"Back to base, then?" said Nicole, a small bubble of hope lifting her leaden tone.

"*Si*," said Sister Margaret. "Let's go."

Amy led the way through the maze of hallways. Thank goodness for stitchers and their fantastic memories. Amy was even better than most, especially considering she hadn't lived here in over a year.

Finally, they reached the antechamber outside their library room, and Amy reached for the doorknob.

Sister Margaret shot out a hand with lightning speed to forestall her.

Amy stared at her with wide, startled eyes, and Sister Margaret dropped her hand, lifting a finger to her lips.

Into the silence, a tenor chuckle came from inside the library.

"Who is that?" Nicole hissed.

Sister Margaret jerked her head and led the way back around the corner. "Are you sure this is the right room?" she asked Amy, keeping her voice low.

"We've seen a lot of hallways that looked really similar," Nicole pointed out.

"I'm sure," said Amy. "Like ninety-nine percent sure."

"That's not quite enough percents," said Sister Margaret.

"The other rooms," said Nicole. "Let's look into the other rooms in the alcove. It's supposed to be a dusty tattoo studio and a little-used workroom."

Amy turned and led the way back around the bend, opening up the door to the right. "Huh."

Sister Margaret peered over Amy's shoulder into the room, which was dominated by a large tattoo chair. "Tattoo parlor. Check."

"Yeah, but–" Amy walked into the room and Sister Margaret followed. "I poked my head in here earlier, just to check it out, and this was different." She touched the chair. "This was positioned at a more reclined angle."

Nicole pointed to the cabinet that sat next to the chair. "Was that ajar before?"

Amy shook her head. "Someone's been in here."

Sister Margaret rubbed her temples. "Look. I'm not saying that this isn't valuable, but it's making my brain hurt. We came in here to figure out one mystery and suddenly there's another one, and it's too many mysteries."

"Well, we solved part of the first mystery anyway," Nicole pointed out. "This is the correct hallway."

"So, who the fuck is in the room with Tillie?" asked Sister Margaret.

"It didn't sound like Trevor," said Amy.

"It kind of sounded like Giovani," said Nicole. "Maybe he was able to get in after all."

Sister Margaret snapped her fingers. "He knew where we were planning to hole up. It would make the most sense for him to head there."

"How would he have known how to get there?" asked Amy. "He's never been in the bunker before."

"I don't know," said Nicole. "But I think the only way to find out is to go inside."

Nicole turned to head back out into the alcove, and Sister Margaret followed close behind her. "We should still be cautious," she warned. "Giovani is the best guess, but it doesn't mean we're right."

Nicole nodded and grasped the door knob, turning it slowly and silently. She slowly pushed open the door and Sister Margaret jumped as it let out a haunted-sounding creak.

"Fuck it," she muttered. She reached into her side sheaths and pulled out her stiletto knives, which would be better in such close quarters than her swords, nudged Nicole aside, and kicked in the door.

Three surprised faces stared at her from the seating area.

Trevor sat frozen with a bottle of water halfway to his lips.

Tillie had jumped to her feet and stood in a martial arts ready position. What was it she practiced again? Some kind of Middle Eastern thing.

Sister Margaret pointed one of her knives at the other person in the room. "Who the fuck is this?" she demanded.

Tillie relaxed and Trevor lowered his water bottle, his eyebrows raised, a small smile tugging at the corners of his mouth. "Coyote, Sister Margaret," he said. "Sister Margaret, Coyote."

Sister Margaret sheathed her knives and crossed her arms, glaring at Trevor. "Where the fuck did you come from? We're supposed to be rescuing you, you know."

"Please consider me rescued," said Trevor, in that mild way of his that somehow managed to oscillate between soothing and infuriating.

Nicole pushed her way past Sister Margaret and collapsed onto an easy chair. "Clearly nothing is fucked here, so can we just sit down and rest, and maybe eat a little something?"

Tillie knelt beside Sister Margaret's backpack and pulled out a bag of jerky, tossing it to Nicole who caught it easily.

"Thanks."

Next, Tillie pulled out three more water bottles and distributed them.

Sister Margaret took hers gratefully and made her way to another chair.

Amy took the last one beside her and reached over to snag some jerky from Nicole's bag. "Okay, there's a story here," she said. "Let's hear it."

***

The tires squealed as Chameleon turned into the parking lot at the only motel in La Panne, Utah. Mattie clutched at the handle as they narrowly missed a telephone pole and slammed into a parking space.

"That seemed unnecessary," said Sammy in a choked voice from the back.

Mattie agreed, but something had gotten into Chameleon ever since meeting up with Raccoon, and she had been unable to get her to tell her exactly what it was. All she knew was that the woman had driven like a crazy person and they'd arrived an hour earlier than the GPS had predicted.

Mattie undid her seatbelt, opened the car door, and jumped out. Oddly enough, Chameleon was still seated, belt on and the car still running. As Mattie watched, Chameleon brought her hand up to her mouth, stopping herself just in time to keep from biting it again.

Stooping to peer back into the car, Mattie furrowed her brow. "You okay? You're in such a hurry until we get here, now you're just gonna sit there?"

Chameleon nodded, lowering her hand. She crossed her wrists, digging the fingernails of both hands into her opposite outer forearms and slowly scratching up and down. She drew in a ragged breath before responding. When she finally did, her voice was deep and raspy, with an odd transatlantic inflection. "Sorry. Give me a moment, please, would ya?"

Mattie nodded. "Honestly, we probably can't make any moves until tomorrow anyway, right? I'll just see if I can get a hold of Giovani, see what room he's in."

"Isn't that Giovani?" said Sammy.

Mattie straightened up and turned around. Sammy was standing on the other side of the car, pointing off into the distance at a figure walking down the sidewalk toward them.

Squinting, Mattie could see Giovani's signature beige suit. She walked into the middle of the sidewalk and waved her arms.

Giovani's pace sped up and he arrived a minute later. "Hey," he said. "I'm glad you're here."

"We came as fast as we could," Mattie said.

"Faster than most people would be willing to drive," Sammy muttered.

Mattie glanced at Chameleon, who seemed to have pulled herself together. Chameleon gave her a small, tight smile and got out of the car.

"See here, we got here in one piece, didn't we?" said Chameleon, tartly. "Don't get your knickers in a bunch."

"Listen," said Giovani, turning to Chameleon. "Do you know an imposing gentleman who lives in town, goes by the name Gonzalez?"

Chameleon stiffened and crossed her wrists again, just holding onto her forearms this time. "How old?"

"Older than me," said Giovani. "But not elderly."

"Wolf," she said. Her hands formed claws against her arms. When she spoke again, her voice had changed once more, back to the Southern belle character. "What happened with Wolf?"

Giovani blinked at her, but didn't comment on the vocal change. "Nothing really," he said. He told them about his evening and his encounter with the man.

As he spoke, Chameleon relaxed gradually until she finally dropped her arms to her side as he finished his story.

"That's Coyote's dad, right?" said Mattie. "He's not on our side."

"Correct," said Chameleon in her regular voice. "Wolf is loyal to the organization, although he is also resentful of them. He feels that he should have been able to choose to be a Special instead of being forced into it. He would have made another decision, lived the life of a high courtier, which he feels is his birthright. It's a dangerous combination." She began to pace. "On the one hand, he thinks if he proves himself often enough, my father will bring him back into the court and he can retire to the life he thinks he deserves. On the other, that little bit of resentment gives him a small piece of unpredictability. There have been times, here and there, where he has acted against the organization because of that. But there's no knowing when or how he will do that."

"And now he knows we're here," said Mattie.

"He knows Giovani is here," Chameleon corrected. "You didn't tell him you were waiting for friends, did you?"

Giovani shook his head. "But he might know that I was with other people before. The bartender remembered that I was part of a group."

"Are Wolf and the bartender friendly?" asked Chameleon.

Laughing, Giovani shook his head again. "Pretty sure that bartender can't stand him, and he was not very nice to her either."

Chameleon nodded. "Good. Coyote has said that his father has made few, if any, friends in this town which is to our advantage. We may be able to just take out Wolf first and then head to the bunker after."

"Take him out?" said Sammy. "I didn't sign up for any assassinations."

Chameleon pinned him in her gaze and he squirmed. "You signed up for battle, did you not? Did you not think you'd be killing anyone?"

Sammy took a step back. "I didn't really think of it in those terms," he said.

"I suggest you start," said Chameleon. "And make a decision by morning whether you want to be a part of this fight or not." She turned to Giovani. "Now. We are tired and need rest. Which room is yours?"

Giovani pointed to a door. "There are two beds. We've been taking turns sleeping in them or on the floor."

Chameleon frowned. "Not ideal. We'll book another room so there is a bed for each of us. I will room with you. I have more questions about Wolf."

Mattie cocked her head. It felt a little counterintuitive that they wouldn't break up the rooms by gender, but then again it wasn't like she needed to worry about Sammy trying anything.

She shrugged and followed the arrow pointing toward the office.

14.

Tillie slept on the floor, snuggled up against Trevor on a soft rug, covered in a blanket they'd taken from her old cell. She dreamed about the first mage she'd ever fought, a bully who had been threatening her friend Stephanie's family's magic shop.

In the dream, she vanquished him quickly and easily, single-handedly. In real life, she had been green and still learning, and it had been a series of skirmishes. In real life, she'd fought alongside Stephanie and several other mages, including the formidable Ida Garaveldi, setting traps for the man over the course of months before they finally ran him out of town.

Tillie woke up briefly, snuggled closer to her best friend, and went back to sleep, dreaming of other long-ago battles.

***

Trevor woke up the next morning to find himself entangled with Tillie, her arms wrapped around his waist, legs entwined, hair dangerously close to his mouth.

He gently moved her hair aside and smiled down at her peaceful, still sleeping face. He was glad to have found her once again., glad they were together and that she was safe again, at least for the moment.

Tillie's eyes fluttered open and his smile widened. "Good morning," he murmured.

"Hello, love," she said sleepily. "Fancy meeting you here."

Trevor chuckled. "In a bunker belonging to an evil secret society. Yeah, that is a bit of a departure from the norm, isn't it?"

"Ever so slightly." Tillie sat up and stretched, twisting to and fro and then reaching clasped hands up into the air above her head and from side to side. She jumped smoothly to her feet and began to stretch out her entire body.

Trevor raised his eyebrows. He and Tillie were the same age, but she remained as nimble as they'd been in their twenties, while he – well. Standing up from the floor took him a little bit longer, and involved a few low groans and also some popping sounds from various joints.

When he was finally vertical, he grimaced at her. She was in the midst of a complicated yoga pose, standing on her left foot with her other leg bent and her right foot resting against her left thigh. "Show off," he whispered.

"You take the same yoga classes I do," she whispered back. "You just don't show up often enough."

Trevor noticed Sister Margaret and Amy stirring in their own sleeping nests, and he jerked his head toward the door.

Tillie followed him out into the hall, where she resumed her routine. Trevor did his best to follow along, and he did feel better when at last they finished, seated on the hard concrete floor, legs crossed, heads bowed, hands pressed together in front of their hearts.

Then the cold began to seep through his cotton trousers and he clambered to his feet once again. "Thank you," he said. "I needed that. I should wake up that way more often."

Tillie smirked. "Told you so."

"You sure have," he admitted.

The door opened and Sister Margaret poked her head out into the hall, her long black hair floating loose around her face. "Breakfast?" she offered, holding out a couple of foil-wrapped energy bars.

"Thank you." Trevor took them both and handed one to Tillie.

Sister Margaret withdrew back into the library.

Trevor tore open the top of the package and lifted his bar to Tillie. "Cheers."

She grinned and tapped her bar against his. "Big day ahead of us," she said. "Today we find out if we're trapped in this bunker forever or if we can get out of here and join the others."

He bit into the chewy, oddly homogenous slab of processed grains and protein. "I'd say it's about fifty-fifty odds either way. Which are you hoping for?"

Tillie pulled a face. "Oh, I would just love to live underground and subsist on semi-nutritious cardboard for the rest of my life."

"On the plus side, though, it probably wouldn't be that long," Trevor pointed out. "If we are stuck in here, we'll almost certainly be either recaptured or killed after a day or two."

"That's what I love about you, Trevs," said Tillie. "You're such an optimist."

***

Mattie awoke to the sound of the motel room door slamming shut.

"Rise and shine, betch," said Sammy. His voice contained unfortunate levels of cheeriness, considering the sun was barely peeking its way through the chinks in the blinds.

"What the fuck time is it?" asked Mattie, sitting up and blinking at him.

"Six o'clock!" he announced as though that was a perfectly reasonable time to get up.

"You're a college kid," Mattie reminded him. "That means you're supposed to be sleeping until noon."

He shrugged. "I took a gap year. I'm twenty-three years old, and technically a grown-up. I'm past that phase."

"Well, I'm thirty-four and I'm not," said Mattie. She sighed and swung her legs off the bed. "Is that breakfast?" She nodded toward the bag Sammy had set down on the table. It did smell good, and she was even more pleased to see two insulated paper cups sitting beside it.

"It sure is." Sammy opened up the bag and rummaged around. "From the cafe next door. Bagel sandwich for you. . . ." He pulled out a paper-wrapped parcel and handed it to her.

"Oh, yum." The sandwich was warm, and she eagerly peeled it open, taking a blissful bite of the sliced everything bagel with egg, spinach, and bacon stuffed in the middle. "Is there mustard on this? I love it," she mumbled with her mouth full.

"Yep! And I also remembered that you're a tea person, so this is your chai latte," said Sammy, handing her one of the cups.

"You're amazing," she said. She swallowed her food and took a careful sip of the chai, closing her eyes as the frothy, creamy spiced tea washed over her tongue. She opened her eyes. "I take it all back."

"Take what back?" said Sammy, pausing with his own sandwich halfway to his lips.

"All of the horrible things I wished upon you when you woke me up," said Mattie. She set down her chai to let it cool a little more and devoted her full attention to the food.

"Well, Chameleon says we're meeting up with Elephant, Raccoon, and a bunch of other animal people in just a few minutes anyway," said Sammy. "So, I'm guessing you'd rather have me wake you up with breakfast than her come charging in here, probably expecting you to be ready to go."

"You spoke with her already?" said Mattie.

"Well, yeah, I dropped off their breakfast before I came back here," said Sammy. "Giovani is as bad as you are, but Chameleon had him already up and dressed anyway." He eyed Mattie's plaid pajama bottoms and nerdy t-shirt. "You're probably going to want to make yourself a bit more presentable before she gets here."

Mattie shrugged. "I'm not worried about presentable." She polished off the last bite of her breakfast and picked up the chai again. "But I should probably be closer to ready-for-action. You're right."

She picked up her backpack, slung it over one shoulder, and strolled into the bathroom.

Setting down her tea, she studied herself in the mirror. "Presentable? I look fine," she told her reflection. Sure, her hair was a little messy – she pulled out a brush and ran it over the long red tresses before scraping it back into a tight braid – and obviously she wasn't going into battle in her jammies.

She got out her jeans and rifled through the backpack for a clean pair of undies and a new shirt. "Why does the underwear always sink to the bottom?" she wondered aloud.

Sammy knocked on the door. "Did you say something to me?" he called.

"No, I'm talking to the gremlin who lives behind the toilet," she called back. "Please don't eavesdrop on our private conversation."

There was a moment of silence from the other side of the door before Sammy finally said, "Look, I feel like you're probably kidding, but also if magic is a thing, maybe toilet gremlins are too?"

"I'm kidding," she said.

"'Kay."

Mattie chuckled and quickly finished changing, splashed some water on her face, brushed her teeth, and exited the bathroom.

Sammy raised an eyebrow. "That was fast."

"I'm not one of those women who takes a zillion years to get ready," Mattie said with a shrug. "Never have been, never will be."

She took a sip of her chai and wrinkled her nose as the flavor of the tea mingled with the aftertaste of her toothpaste.

Somebody knocked urgently on the door and kept on knocking until Sammy reached over and flung it open.

Chameleon strode into the room and surveyed the two of them. She was in full armor. "What is this?" she demanded.

Mattie stared at her. "What?"

"You're only half dressed, sitting around eating breakfast like a languid high courtier with nowhere to be?" She pounded her fist on the table.

Mattie jumped.

"Hey," she said. "Settle down. You know I'm on board with the gravity of this whole situation, but we've been driving cross country for two days, and it's important to be at our best."

Chameleon leaned forward on the table, her eyes narrowing. "Today, we go to war."

"And I'm not going into war without a good breakfast first," said Mattie. Holding eye contact with Chameleon, she took a long, deliberate drink from her chai and then set down the cup on her nightstand. "Tired, hungry people make mistakes. I don't want to die today because I'm not at the top of my game."

Chameleon's nostrils flared, but she pursed her lips and nodded once, curtly. "Fair point. You are not as accustomed as I am to pushing yourself for days on end."

Mattie sighed. "Look, Chameleon, I hope that after this is over, you won't feel like you have to do that anymore."

Chameleon blinked at her. "After this is over?" she said, slowly. She sat down heavily on Mattie's bed and laughed mirthlessly. "This will be over someday," she said.

"Maybe soon," said Mattie, gently. "That hadn't occurred to you?"

"What will you do with yourself?" Sammy asked.

"I don't know," said Chameleon.

"That can be decided later," said a girlish voice from the doorway.

Mattie looked up to see Raccoon and Elephant lounging there, looking very confident and bad-ass in their leather armor. Raccoon even had war paint on her face, which, combined with her shaved head, gave her the appearance of a character from a post-apocalyptic movie.

Even the petite Elephant looked fierce, her armor covered in spikes and plenty of visible weaponry. Mattie was willing to bet there were more weapons hidden too.

"We're not going into the bunker right away, though, right?" asked Sammy. "We're supposed to be confronting this Wolf person."

Chameleon nodded and stood, walking toward Raccoon and Elephant. "Weren't there any other Specials in town?"

"More foes than friends, I'm afraid, but yes." Raccoon began ticking them off on her fingers. "Meerkat, Crocodile, Hawk, Rattlesnake."

"Hyena is on her way," Elephant interjected. "And I have reason to believe that Cheetah, Weasel, and Grizzly are already inside, guarding the Pontiff."

"Of course they are," Chameleon growled. "Fortunately, it would seem that Wolf's claim of being already inside was exaggerated, so we have a chance to head him off before he becomes a threat."

"Or convert him to our side," said Raccoon.

"What?" Chameleon frowned. "I don't think so."

Mattie sipped her chai, fascinated by the conversation and trying to remember which of the four Raccoon had named were initially on the friend or the foe list she and Chameleon had made.

"Have you met any of these people?" asked Sammy in a low voice.

Mattie started. She hadn't realized Sammy had circled around to stand next to her. She shook her head and Sammy sat down next to her, where Chameleon had been sitting a minute ago. "Anyone named after an animal that doesn't eat chickens is on our side," she said. "Except Coyote. I mean, Coyotes eat chickens, but he's on our side. I never did quite figure out why he was exempt from that."

"That's the weirdest code I've ever heard, but okay," said Sammy.

She shrugged. "Their names seem to be based on their skills or their personality, so maybe it's just that the gentler names, the ones that aren't meat-eaters, are more likely to be given to the kinds of people likely to object to an organization that kidnaps and brainwashes people."

"You guys know we can hear you, right?" said Elephant. "You could just ask us directly instead of talking about us like we're not here."

"Sorry," said Mattie. "He started it."

"What about Bonobo?" asked Chameleon. "We need her."

Elephant shrugged. "I left her a message. I can't imagine she isn't either here or on her way. Everyone knows this is where it's happening."

"And that it's happening now," added Raccoon.

"All right," said Chameleon. "Where are Meerkat and Rattlesnake, then?"

"I'm here," said a new voice from outside. A slender man finagled his way deftly between Raccoon and Elephant and presented himself before Chameleon with a jaunty salute. "Reporting for duty, my liege."

Mattie was willing to bet a solid gold nugget that this was Meerkat. He had a very perky, meerkat kind of vibe.

"At ease, soldier," said Chameleon with a smile. "And Rattlesnake?"

"I knew it," Mattie muttered.

"Wait, why is Rattlesnake on our side?" said Sammy. "Don't they eat chickens?"

"According to the internet, they can, but they tend to stick to eggs," Mattie informed him.

"I have spoken to Rattlesnake," said Meerkat, still standing at attention. "She has pressing business inside, but will meet us there as soon as we get word to her that we are inside as well."

Chameleon nodded. "Then we should go. Mattie, Sammy, arm up, please."

"Where's Giovani?" asked Mattie as she stood and walked to the closet where she had stashed her armor and weapons the night before.

"He was still preparing himself when I left the room," said Chameleon.

"I'll go grab him," said Sammy. "I don't have any armor anyway."

"You need armor," said Elephant. "Especially if you're going to be fighting alongside us. We're heading straight into the thick of things once we're inside. You'll be up against some very formidable opponents."

"Probably better you wait for the rest of the army," said Mattie. "You're barely trained anyway."

"Nevertheless," said Meerkat. "Armor is important for battle." He looked Sammy up and down. "We are of a size. You may borrow some of mine."

Sammy smirked. "I don't mind getting into your armor."

Meerkat looked him up and down once again. "You are much younger than I am."

"So?"

Meerkat shrugged. "Sometimes that bothers people outside the organization. I have no real objection. Let's see if we survive this."

Sammy grinned.

Mattie shook her head. She supposed that if you just went around hitting on every human male in a twelve-mile radius, eventually one of them would respond positively. It really was a numbers game.

***

Tillie was dressed in Nicole's clothing, which was very nice of Nicole to give her, even if everything was ever-so-slightly too long. But at least it was flattering and functional, and nobody had brought any extra armor, so she hadn't had to figure out a way to bow out of wearing that.

Mattie may have bought into the whole movie-assassin look, but she would rather be able to move properly. Better to feel comfortable and able to dodge any blows that came at her than weighted down and more likely to get hit.

Then again, without seer sight, she was already more likely to get hit. Tillie shrugged. It was a moot point. Nobody had brought along extra armor.

She studied herself in the mirror and nodded at her reflection. She would do.

Tillie exited the bathroom of her former cell and headed back up the hall, opening the door of the library only to find it empty. Frowning, she turned around.

She could hear voices from somewhere, so she opened up the central door in the alcove, the one that led to a workroom. Sure enough, there she found everyone, huddling around a scrying stone on an altar in the middle of the room.

Trevor beckoned her in and then turned his attention back to the stone, which was glowing.

Apparently somebody was able to scry.

Tillie hurried forward, stepping up beside Trevor, who inched aside to make room for her. Peering into the stone, she saw a tiny room full of guards. "What am I looking at?" she asked.

"The door out," said Trevor.

"How are we looking at it?" she said. "I thought all magery was dampened."

Coyote lifted his shirt to show a row of tattoos and then lowered it, but nobody said anything, just kept staring into the stone.

Tillie waited for another beat, but still nobody spoke. "Is that supposed to mean something to me?" she asked.

"His tattoos are keyed to the defense spell," said Trevor. "He can do magic."

"Fantastic!" said Tillie. "How do I get in on that?"

Coyote finally spoke, the stone darkening as his eyes went from blank white to ordinary. "I don't have enough ink to do all of you," he said, regretfully. "After doing Trevor's ink–"

Tillie smacked Trevor in the arm.

"Hey!" he said.

"Sorry. I didn't hit you that hard."

"Why did you hit me at all?" he protested.

"I've been trying to convince you to get tattoos with me for years!"

"I pretty much bullied him into it," said Coyote. "Anyway, I didn't realize there would be so many of you. I think I could do one tat each."

"How many did Trevor get?" she demanded.

"Three," Trevor admitted.

She considered smacking him on the arm again, but she figured she'd made her point. "How do they work?"

"Since Trevor is a natural stitcher and not truly trained in morphing I gave him the ones that allow stitching and spelling, but not seeing. And I gave him the one that will prevent seers from seeing him."

Tillie whistled softly. "That is a nice trick. As a seer I'm a little torn on the idea, but I bet it comes in handy."

"Just so we're clear," said Coyote. "It won't work if the seer has this tattoo." He lifted his shirt again and pointed to one of his, a sigil that looked like a horseshoe with three crosses at the top and some random small circles distributed throughout. "So, any of the Specials will still be able to see him, but not the guards. Most of the courtiers don't have this one either."

"I'll take the seeing sigil," said Tillie.

"I think we should each get the sigil for our own natural discipline," said Sister Margaret. "I sure would love to be able to see again when I'm fighting these bastards."

"Fair enough," said Coyote. "One at a time." He pointed to Tillie. "You're first. The rest of you, figure out where you want it, and then get rid of the armor covering that spot."

***

Mattie marched between Sammy and Giovani at the rear of the group as they moved en masse – behind a sight shield, lest the locals get weird about it – toward the mechanic shop that Wolf used as his front in order to maintain a presence in the town that hid Broken Bunker.

She felt a little bit disoriented. If she was a math teacher instead of English, she would probably have worked out the statistical probability at some point of how staggeringly unlikely it was that while driving across the country to seek out her sister, who was on the run from the Auditors, she had ended up getting her car looked at by a mechanic who was a spy for said Auditors.

At least she wasn't confronting the same mechanic – just his dad.

For a moment, she found herself thinking about her old boss, Jill, who had been a math teacher before being promoted to vice-principal. She wondered if Jill was still looking for Dr. Alvarez, the principal, or if he'd ever shown up again. She suspected not, since he had turned out to also be an Auditor spy.

Shaking off thoughts of the past, Mattie stared at the pommel of the broadsword that Raccoon carried on her back. She was unsurprised to see that there was an occult symbol decorating it, but she was a little surprised to realize that she recognized the symbol. It was the same one that Ida had shown her in Trevor's house, the one that Trevor had recognized from a book of medieval secret societies. A symbol of the organization they were fighting against.

But officially, Raccoon was part of that organization. So were Elephant and Meerkat.

Mattie wondered if Chameleon was still considered part of the organization or if she'd been declared rogue yet. Last she'd heard, Chameleon was "missing, presumed captured."

Elephant and Chameleon stopped suddenly, and Mattie almost stumbled into Raccoon's back, stopping herself just in time. Sammy grabbed her arm to steady himself, and she gave him a small smile.

Mattie looked around, trying to figure out why they'd stopped. Then she spotted the man who was standing in front of the familiar mechanic shop, smoking a cigarette.

"What the fuck?" she yelped. Speaking of incredibly unlikely....

Giovani, Sammy, and the three Specials turned to look at her.

"I know that guy, " she said. "That's Dr. Alvarez."

15.

Tillie chose to have her tattoo placed on her left hip, directly opposite the seer sigil she had on her right hip. She showed Coyote the other tattoo so he could match the size and they would be uniform.

As she lay on the tattoo chair, which Coyote had adjusted to a more comfortable setting for the way she'd be laying, she sort of wished Trevor had also turned out to be a seer, so they would finally have matching tattoos.

Maybe at some point in the future she could get one of the ones he'd gotten, and they would match. If they both survived. And if their friendship survived.

She thought it would. They had had a good talk after their piano duet. Coyote had disappeared for a while to give them some privacy, and they'd discussed everything, tears and all. It had been wonderfully cathartic.

They could never go back to the special closeness they'd had, but maybe that was a good thing.

Their closeness, in a lot of ways, had been an illusion once it had included her hiding a major part of her life from him. Now they could move on to a better friendship, even closer than ever before, an evolution beyond brunches and exercise classes, more like a mature version of what they'd had as kids.

As the glowing needle buzzed against her skin, she felt a small euphoria. She wasn't sure if it was the rush of the tattoo gun or the thrill of thinking of a better future. Probably a little of each.

Tillie glanced down and saw that the sigil was almost complete. She looked at the clock; it was a small piece but incredibly intricate, and it had taken about half an hour. "Wow," she said. "You're fast."

"I've done this for a lot of my friends," Coyote said absently. "All of the Specials have them, and we're all trained to do them, but just like anything else, some are better at it than others. I've always had a certain talent for it."

He wiped the area clean and leaned back to give it a critical look. "I think we're done," he said. "Let me get the space cleaned up a little and then give you some ointment, and you can head out and send the next one in."

***

Everyone stared at Mattie for a long moment. Finally, Chameleon nodded. "Alverez is one of his cover identities."

"He's very proud of his doctorate and will go by 'Dr.' whenever possible," Raccoon added.

"But when did you encounter him?" asked Chameleon. "If not when you were in this town before?"

Mattie shook her head. "He was my boss in Portland. The principal of my school."

"Ah." Elephant nodded. "That's common practice," she explained. "One of our jobs as Special Agents has been to run surveillance on friends and relatives of new recruits before and during extraction, especially people who are close to the recruit or who are also mages or who are just generally considered a possible complication."

"They weren't wrong," Giovani pointed out. "You and Trevor did end up causing complications when you went after Tillie."

"You caused as much complication as I did, if not more," Mattie pointed out.

"But I didn't know Tillie in advance," said Giovani. "She just happened to be on the agenda when I decided to leave."

"Do you know if there were any Specials assigned to Trevor as well?" asked Chameleon.

Mattie shrugged. "I didn't know there was one assigned to me until just now. How would I know about Trevor?"

"We'll cross that bridge when we come to it. In the meantime, I vote we send Mattie in first," said Raccoon. "Catch him off-guard, and then while he's trying to figure out what she's doing there, we swoop in and take him out."

Mattie nodded. "Damn, I hated that guy."

"He is an undeniable ass," said Meerkat.

"So, what do I do?" said Mattie.

"Go in and say you're looking for his son, Jorge. I'm sure he knows about the random woman who left her belongings here a couple of months ago," said Chameleon. "He'll be shocked to discover you are that woman, but it will be perfectly normal for you to be returning."

"Right." Mattie squared her shoulders and stepped forward.

"Wait!" said Sammy. "You don't look like some random woman."

"What?" Mattie turned and frowned at him. "What do you mean?"

"You're wearing leather armor," he said. "He'll know you're all maged out now."

"He knows that anyway," Chameleon pointed out. "It's our job as Specials to know these things. He absolutely knows that Mattie and Tillie Holiday are ringleaders in the Fox organization. He just doesn't know that Mattie Holiday is the one who left her things with Coyote."

Mattie paused. She was having a little trouble following that. "So, I'm good to keep the armor on."

"Yes," said Chameleon. "But I applaud your initiative, young man. It was a good point to make."

Sammy grinned and gave her two thumbs up.

Turning, Mattie continued toward the mechanic shop. Wolf had finished his smoke break while they'd been conferring, and was no longer outside, so she headed for the glass front door. Peering inside, she didn't see anyone in the waiting area.

Good. There were no innocents just waiting for an oil change to get caught in the crossfires.

She reached for the metal bar and pulled the door open. A bell above the door jingled and a familiar chilly baritone voice called out, "I'll be right there."

Despite the muggy summer air, Mattie shivered.

She took a deep breath. Dr. Alvarez was dangerous, more dangerous than most of the opponents she'd faced before now, and while her friends were as formidable as he was, they wouldn't be rushing in to save her for another few minutes.

A lot could happen in a few minutes, especially between mages.

She paced the small waiting room, which looked and smelled just like every mechanic shop waiting room. A row of cracked blue adjoined plastic chairs lined the large window across from a desk. The desktop was dominated by a large calendar with fake leather corners holding it down and scrawls across many of the dates. Surrounding the calendar were several metal spikes with stacks of hand-written receipts of varying sizes pinned to them.

A small alarm clock, the old-fashioned kind with two brass bells on top, sat incongruously at the edge, facing outward.

Finally, she heard heavy footsteps from the adjacent garage, and she spun around to face the mage who was entering the waiting room.

Wolf didn't look at her as he hurried over to the desk, wiping his hands on a rag. "Let's see here," he said, running a finger down the calendar squares. "I don't see any appointments right now. Are you dropping off your car, Ms–"

He finally looked up and his eyes widened as he took her in.

Mattie crossed her arms and raised her eyebrows.

"–Holiday," he finished. "Well, well, well. Mathilda. You found me."

"Actually, I'm just here for my things," she said. "Is your son around? Jorge, I believe he said his name was?"

Wolf frowned. "Jorge? You're looking for Jorge?"

"I left all of my earthly possessions with him. I was driving through town, you see, on my way to find *my sister*, when my car broke down."

"I– Um–" Wolf stammered. "*You're* the lady whose things we've been keeping?"

Mattie nodded. "And I'd like them back now."

"Now?" he said. "Right now? In the middle of– You want your things back?"

"That's right." Mattie stifled a grin. After all the running around she'd had to do on his behalf when he'd been her boss, it was actually pretty fun to flummox the hell out of the man. "I mean, I'm in town for the siege anyway."

"Aha!" he said.

Mattie snorted. She'd never heard anyone actually say that unironically.

"So there is to be a siege?" he said, pointing at her as though she'd let some huge secret out.

"Well, yeah," she said. "What did you think we'd do? Surely you're aware that we've got an army on the way here."

"Of course," he said. "Everyone knows that."

He was starting to sound more confident now. She needed to get him back to off-kilter before Chameleon and the others arrived. Where were they, anyway? She thought they'd be attacking by now.

"Well, why aren't you inside the bunker, then?" she asked.

"I don't want to be under a siege," he said.

"So you did know there was a siege," she countered.

"Um." Good, he was back to being confused. "I thought I already said that I knew that."

Oh, yeah.

Just then, the door behind her shattered with a crash.

Mattie hit the deck, erecting a mage shield as she threw herself at the floor. A couple of shards of glass still got through. Most of them hit her armor, but she felt sharp pain from her cheek as one of them cut her.

Looking up, she saw that Wolf hadn't been as prepared, and his face and arms were bloody with small cuts.

Scrambling to her hands and knees, Mattie crawled out of the way as Chameleon, Elephant, Raccoon, and Meerkat began to unleash spell after spell on Wolf's hastily constructed shields.

"Wait!" Wolf shouted. He was making no effort to fight back, just holding his shields firm, and he raised his arms over his head. "Wait, please."

The others paused and looked toward Chameleon, who narrowed her eyes but gave a curt nod. "You have thirty seconds to say what you'd like to say," she instructed. "And then we destroy your shields and kill you."

"My son is locked up in there," said Wolf. "I know you love my son. So do I."

Chameleon snorted. "Since when?"

"Always!" Wolf protested. "I don't always show it, I know. But you know where we come from. What we do. How can I be a perfect father in this environment?"

"You had a better chance than most," said Raccoon. "You got to live with Coyote out here." She gestured widely. "It's rare that a Special has the chance to have a child. But as a Special, you should have known better than the rest of the court."

"Maybe I should have, but I didn't," said Wolf. "And I've been realizing it of late."

Chameleon studied him. Abruptly, the glow on her hands pulsed and a floor-to-ceiling wall of energy went up between Wolf and the rest of the Specials.

Probably a sound shield so they could speak without him overhearing.

"I know you want him to be telling the truth," said Meerkat. "Who among us wouldn't die for parental approval for ourselves or our friends?"

Mattie's heart ached. Her parents had died young, but at least they had loved her and Tillie beforehand, and had shown it the best they could, despite living in relative poverty.

"But none of us have had it," Chameleon agreed. "That is our reality, and I think you are correct – Wolf is no exception to this rule."

Raccoon stared in Wolf's direction. "I'm not so sure."

Chameleon's eyebrows shot up. "Really? You, of all of us, are considering trusting Wolf?"

"People have accused me of playing both sides before," said Raccoon.

"That's because you have played both sides before," said Elephant dryly. "Don't think we have forgotten about Prague. Or Detroit. Sidney, Minsk, Havana. Need I continue?"

"No," said Raccoon. "You needn't. But the fact is that I am here now, by your side. When it matters most. Why is that?"

"You know why," said Chameleon.

"Shouldn't Wolf be given the same consideration? I know you haven't forgotten my transgressions. But you've forgiven them, at least enough for this most important of occasions. We may find each other at odds again someday. I do not pretend that isn't possible. But for now, we fight together. If Wolf wishes to fight with us, why should we push him back to our enemy's side?"

Mattie could hear the ticking of the alarm clock in the otherwise silent room as Chameleon considered this. The others stood and watched her.

Her leg was starting to cramp, so Mattie shifted slightly moving from her kneeling position into a cross-legged seat, careful of the broken glass littering the floor around her.

As she moved, Meerkat spun toward her, his hands glowing with an uncast spell. Reflexively, she raised a shield before he could let loose his spell on her.

Meerkat relaxed as he looked at her, lowering his no-longer-glowing hands. He turned back toward Chameleon.

"All right," said Chameleon, finally. She gave no signs of having noticed Mattie moving, or that she had almost been turned into a charcoal briquette by Meerkat.

Mattie exhaled and released her shield.

Chameleon lowered her own shield. "All right," she said again for Wolf's benefit.

Wolf smiled tightly. "Thank you, Princess."

"Don't give me that 'princess' shit," Chameleon snapped. "I know your games. You know that a name has power and you've always striven to call everyone around you the perfect name to frustrate and infuriate them." She stepped forward and leaned over the desk, her face inches from his. "You will call me Chameleon." She began pointing at each person individually and unerringly, without looking at them. "You will call her Raccoon. Meerkat. Mattie. Elephant. There are two men standing guard outside. One is called Giovani and the other is Sammy. You will use those names. And when we get inside the bunker, you will. Call. Your. Son. Coyote."

Wolf straightened his spine, drawing himself up to his full imposing height, but he nodded. "Yes, Chameleon."

"You will do this without any hint of sarcasm, irony, or resentment in your voice," she continued.

"Yes, Chameleon."

"And you will not overuse someone's name in any kind of pointed way."

"Yes, Cha– Yes."

Chameleon pushed herself off the desk. "Good." She bared her teeth in what was technically a smile. "And if I catch a whiff of any insubordination, on that matter or any other, you will die."

Wolf nodded quickly. "Yes. Absolutely."

Chameleon jerked her head toward the door. "Let's go."

"I have customers today," said Wolf.

"I don't give a flying fuck about your customers," said Chameleon. "Lock up your shop. We're–"

Giovani poked his head through the front of the shop where the window used to be. "Incoming," he said. "A guy just pulled into the lot."

"My customer," said Wolf. His hands moved in a stitch and suddenly the window was whole again.

His face and arms were still covered in cuts from the previously-shattered glass, but Mattie noticed that the few shards that had still been stuck in the cuts were now gone. She felt a trickle of blood on her face and realized that she must have also had a piece of glass stuck there.

The stitch essentially put all the glass back the way it had been.

A familiar figure strolled up the door, and Mattie frowned. Where had she seen the kind-faced older gentleman before?

The bell jingled as the door swung open and the man stopped just inside, looking around at the crowded waiting room.

"Hi, Johnny," said Wolf. "I'm sorry, but I was about to close up."

Johnny blinked. "You've never called me Johnny before, Martin."

Wolf glanced at Chameleon. "It's the name you prefer, isn't it?"

"Yeah." He shook his head. "Thanks. I thought I had an appointment, though? Betsy's making that noise again."

At the car's name, Mattie realized where she knew him from. He had been the one who had helped her push her car across the road from the gas station to the mechanic's after it wouldn't start back up again.

Johnny glanced at Mattie, still seated on the floor, and did a double-take. "Hey, I know you. Mattie, right?"

She nodded.

"Did you ever find your sister?"

"Yeah."

"Glad to hear it. Back for your things now?"

"Not exactly," she admitted.

"Ah," he said. He watched her as she grasped the edge of the row of chairs and leveraged herself to her feet. "Here for the siege, then?"

Mattie froze. "Excuse me?"

He gestured toward her feet and upward. "Dressed like that? And based on what I saw when you were here and I took a peek into your future – plus you were headed to St. Louis at the time – I'm going to go out on a limb and say that you're mixed up with either the Foxes or the Harpers."

"You're a Harper," she said, realization dawning. "Lansdowne mentioned an operative here in town."

"Ya got me," he said. "Why else would I still be driving a car with so many problems? Best way to keep an eye on your local mechanic."

"We were just leaving," interrupted Chameleon. "We are going to Broken Bunker. Are you with us or against us?"

"I'm going to have to bow out," said Johnny, seemingly unfazed by Chameleon's abrupt manner. "Army's coming in this afternoon, and I've reserved the entire state park for them. Gotta go do some prep work."

"Today?" said Mattie. "I thought they were a week behind us." This must have been what those texts she'd missed were about.

Johnny shrugged. "Word on the street is that the nuns are eager to get this over with. They called in some favors and got Church mages all along the way to help stitch the vans bit by bit."

"From St. Louis?" said Raccoon. "That must have taken – I don't even know what that would take. How many vans?"

Johnny shrugged. "The Vatican wants something done, they're gonna get it done; you know that. Their resources make the Auditors look like a cub scout troop."

Giovani let out a low whistle. "Glad they're on our side."

"If the army is arriving today, it's that much more urgent that we get into the bunker right away and assess the situation," said Elephant.

Chameleon nodded. "Let's go. Thank you for the information, Johnny."

Johnny smiled. "You betcha." He held the door open and Mattie trailed after the Specials as they marched out in single file.

16.

Tillie looked up as Amy and Coyote walked into the library. Amy was the last to be tattooed, so Tillie jumped to her feet and stretched. Sister Margaret and Nicole grabbed their backpacks as Amy hurried to do the same.

Tillie, Trevor, and Coyote were packless.

A few seconds later, the group was ready to go.

"We won't be able to stitch out of the bunker," Coyote reminded them. "Even those of us now able to stitch. We need to make our way to the physical door, but I'll be able to open it and hold it open for the rest of you, thanks to this little guy right there." He tapped a spot on his side, indicating a specific spelled tattoo.

Sister Margaret took over the instructions. "We'll start by walking. If we run into single or small groups of agents or guards, we'll fight. Try to take out as many as possible – that way there are fewer to fight once the army gets here. If we run into large groups, link arms and Amy will stitch us out, always moving us closer to the door."

"Why Amy?" asked Trevor. "Why not Coyote?"

"Unlike many morphers, I've spent much of my life doing my best to stick as closely to my natural discipline as I can," said Coyote. "Honing my seeing abilities and temperament like that has given me an edge over others within the organization."

Tillie nodded. That made a lot of sense – she had noticed a shift in herself that she wasn't too happy about. Maybe once this was all over, she would pull back from stitching and spelling, only using them when absolutely necessary.

"I'll stitch in a pinch," Coyote added. "But Amy has a clear enough idea of where we're going and she's much more suited to stitching out so many people all at once."

"All right," said Nicole – the only natural speller in the group eager for action of course. "Let's get moving!"

Coyote led the way, turning on his seer sight as he opened the door.

Tillie turned hers on too, filing into the single line behind Trevor and in front of Sister Margaret, who was bringing up the rear.

They made it around the corner and down the first corridor before Coyote lifted a hand to stop them.

Tillie saw why a second later, when her seer sight showed a group of three guards rounding the corner.

She stepped forward, the six of them forming a staggered line across the hallway to block the guards' way.

As soon as the three guards were in front of them, Nicole and Amy let loose with spells and Sister Margaret threw a metal star directly at the throat of the leader. The guards were down within two seconds, and the group silently resumed their single file line and continued down the hall.

***

"If the army is arriving later today, we need to hurry to rescue Tillie and Trevor first," said Mattie. "And get our other people out too."

"Don't you think your other people will have rescued them by now?" said Chameleon. "They've been in for a couple of days now, haven't they?"

"We should be inside anyway," said Raccoon. "The effectiveness of a siege can be so much more when you have groups on both sides of the walls."

"And Rattlesnake is already in there," Meerkat reminded them. "We should join forces with her. The Specials should not be a divided force."

"The Specials are a divided force," said Chameleon. "We are split between loyalties."

"Well, this group of the Specials, then," Meerkat amended. "The Rogue Specials."

"That would be a great band name," said Mattie.

Raccoon grinned. "Perhaps we'll take up music if we survive this."

"You are right," said Chameleon.

Mattie frowned. "About starting a band?"

"About going inside." She narrowed her eyes. "This is not a joking matter."

Raccoon laughed. "Is anything a joking matter to you, though?" She nudged Chameleon gently on the arm. "Some of us have to joke or we'll panic."

"All right," said Chameleon. "Do what you need to do. But we will make our way inside now. Search out the detention wings to make sure the prisoners have been freed. Free them if they have not. And then we will head for the Pontiff's chambers. That is where we can do the most damage. Straight for the heart."

Mattie blinked. Chameleon sounded very calm about the idea of killing her own father. Then again, he hadn't been much of a father to her. It seemed like the Specials were the only true family she had.

"Let's go, then," said Raccoon.

Chameleon led the way, opening the re-assembled door, the jingle of the bell providing a contrast to her combat boots thudding rhythmically against the tile floor and then the concrete outside.

The group fell into a similar formation as before, Mattie in the center of the three non-Specials in the last row behind Meerkat and Raccoon, who in turn marched behind Chameleon.

Wolf marched beside Chameleon.

Mattie expected Chameleon to lead them back to the motel for the car, but instead she turned right, heading up the highway.

They marched on the wide shoulder, a sight shield surrounding them. Nobody in the cars that sped past gave them a second glance.

Mattie's legs and feet were beginning to ache by the time they finally turned onto a gravel lane.

Without speaking, the Specials shifted formation, spreading out across the road.

Mattie looked at Giovani, who shrugged. She looked at Sammy, who gave her a wry smile. The three of them were out of their depth, basically just along for the ride.

Giovani and Sammy moved away from her, mimicking the Specials to spread their line across the narrow lane. Mattie instinctively moved forward as Chameleon had, turning the shape of the group into an arrowhead.

Minutes later, Chameleon turned and stopped at a shallow driveway, like a parking lot at a trailhead, but there was no wooden trail marker.

Instead, a small hillside rose up in front of her – and in the center of the hillside, a round, handle-less door painted tan to match the scrubland surrounding it.

This had to be the bunker.

17.

Coyote held up his hand again in the signal that guards were coming. This was the fourth skirmish they'd had, and the group was falling into a routine, alternating between defenders. Tillie positioned herself in front of Sister Margaret in a ready stance, while beside her, Trevor and Coyote prepared their own defenses.

Amy, Nicole, and Sister Margaret waited behind them, saving their strength in case they were needed.

It seemed the guards patrolled in trios, and this batch was no different. In her mage sight, Tillie saw them round the corner, and then a second later they did so in real life.

She flung herself at the central figure, kicking straight at his temple as Trevor slashed at his opponent with his sword and Coyote threw a small dagger. Their enemies fell quickly, and Tillie lowered her defenses, only to lift her hands again as she caught sight of two more mages in her seer sight.

"Incoming!" she called out. Coyote yelled out a warning of his own at the same time.

Tillie, Trevor, and Coyote fell back as Sister Margaret, Amy, and Nicole pushed forward, their spells or weapons at the ready.

"Wait!" said Tillie, realizing that the two figures coming toward them were dressed, not in guard orange or agent leathers but in slim-cut black suits, similar to the one Trevor was clad in.

"Harpers," said Sister Margaret, lowering her throwing star, but not stowing it away quite yet. "Trevor? You know them, right?"

She grabbed Nicole's hand, and Nicole projected the image of the pair onto the wall beside them.

"Yes, those are the ones who helped me," Trevor confirmed.

Tillie diffused her fireball as the pair of mages came around the bend and stopped short at the sight of them.

The woman's hands glowed, while the man's face broke into a smile and he strode toward Trevor, hand outstretched. "Trevor! You seem to have found some friends. Is one of them the one you were hoping to break free?"

Trevor clasped the man's hand, shaking it, his own face jovial as well. His eyes returned to their deep brown as he tipped head toward Tillie. "Yes, that's her right there. Thank you for all of your help."

"We're heading out of the bunker," said Amy. "To wait for the army. If you'd like to join us."

The woman lowered her hands, but Tillie noticed they still glowed. She wasn't quite willing to trust them entirely. Or maybe she was just concerned about who else might come around the corner.

The man shook his head. "We still have work to do here, and there's value in having people inside. We'll remain here until the final battle begins."

"Suit yourselves," said Sister Margaret. She stowed her throwing star in its pouch flat on her thigh, and pointed down the hall the way they'd been heading. "Let's go, troops."

Moving back into their single file formation, the troops headed down the corridor toward the front door to the bunker.

***

Chameleon's hands glowed and Mattie watched as the door swung slowly open.

"Very Middle Earth," muttered Sammy beside her.

She glanced at him. "Are you sure you want to go in there?" she asked. "This isn't a game, you know."

Sammy's face was uncharacteristically serious. "I understand that. You haven't been a mage much longer than I have, right?"

She nodded. "That's true."

"So you should understand. Now that I know this is real, I can't not participate in it."

"There are other ways to participate in magery than storming this bunker," she said. "My understanding is that many mages go their entire lives without dealing with anything of this magnitude."

"Fair enough," he said. "But I've never been one of those people. I've never been the person who sees something bad happening and goes, 'Oh, I hope someone else fixes that.' I've always stood up to bullies, my own and anyone else's. I've marched for gay rights, been tear-gassed and arrested during BLM riots. I've even broken into cosmetics labs and freed all the bunnies and found homes for them." He smiled. "I kept one from the first time I did that. Her name is Denise Hopper and I still have her. I know you see me as just a kid, and think I don't know what I'm doing, but I've always been a warrior."

Mattie smiled. "In that case, I'm glad to have you fighting at my side."

"Me too," said Giovani.

"Are you ready?" asked Chameleon. "Something's happened. There should be guards attacking us, but nobody is here."

Oh, yeah, that was odd, now that Mattie thought about it. This bunker was supposed to be impossibly impenetrable.

"Yeah, we're ready," said Giovani.

The four Specials led the way inside, the three others trailing behind.

Mattie tried to turn on her seer sight, but nothing happened – there must be a spell preventing magery.

Suddenly, she saw a furtive figure slip through the door that stood ajar right in front of them, and she drew her sword.

She lowered her weapon as the Specials began to smile and the figure came out into the light.

The person turned out to be a tall graceful middle-aged Black woman with short spiky hair that was dyed pink. She had several facial piercings and her cheekbones were adorned with tribal tattoos.

The way she moved told Mattie that this could be nobody else but Rattlesnake.

"Welcome, comrades," she said, her voice rich and velvety.

Mattie felt immediately comfortable in her presence.

The woman opened her arms and all four Specials stepped forward for a group hug. Rattlesnake eyed Mattie and her friends with twinkling eyes. "You may join in if you wish. I won't bite you."

Sammy didn't hesitate, but flung himself forward into the huddle. Mattie and Giovani exchanged glances.

Mattie didn't want to intrude, so she gave Rattlesnake a small smile and then walked over to the door she'd come through and peeked out. More dead guards littered the antechamber.

Mattie turned around and saw that the group hug was pulling apart.

Giovani hadn't joined in – he was just standing awkwardly off to the side.

"Tell us what is happening," said Chameleon.

"A lot, actually," said Rattlesnake with a grin. "I've been doing my part to keep this door clear. They stopped sending new guards two rotations ago, as I've been lying in wait every time. They tried to take me out, sending in a good dozen or so, but as your friend can see–" she nodded toward Mattie, who still stood at the door "– I took care of those. Why they didn't send any Specials to fight a Special . . . ? Well, the court has always been populated by idiots."

"They've got the Specials guarding the Pontiff, I would imagine," said Elephant. "He won't care about the rest of the bunker, as long as he himself is safe."

"That's right," said Rattlesnake. "And they're all in there, the cowards. Crocodile, Hyena, Cheetah, Weasel, and Hawk."

"Hawk," said Wolf. "Hawk is here?"

Rattlesnake's eyebrows rose. "Did the two of you have a falling out? I'm surprised to see you here and not in there with her."

Wolf's face closed itself off. "She has chosen her side, and I've chosen mine."

"Fair enough," said Rattlesnake. "I think you've chosen well."

"Do you know where Bonobo is?" asked Meerkat.

Rattlesnake frowned. "I haven't heard from her. This is troubling."

"Maybe we should wait," said Elephant. "As of right now, we have stronger numbers, but only just. Bonobo would tip us over firmly into a majority."

"The army of Foxes, Harpers, and Church Warrior Mages arrives this afternoon," said Chameleon. "They will not waste time. The Harper in town is preparing them a base at the park."

"Early afternoon or late afternoon?" asked Rattlesnake. "Even just an hour may make the difference between whether they attack today or wait until tomorrow."

"I think it's better to assume early," said Giovani.

Rattlesnake smiled, showing teeth that appeared pointier than normal teeth. "And you are . . . ?"

He lifted his chin. "Giovani Garaveldi," he said. "A leader among the Foxes."

"Welcome to Broken Bunker," she said. "I am Rattlesnake, a leader among the Auditors' Special agents."

Giovani held her gaze.

Finally her smile widened. "I like this one. A leader, indeed. You have knowledge of this army and its habits?"

"It's a brand new army," said Mattie. "No real habits have been formed yet." She forestalled Rattlesnake's intimidation tactics by sticking out a hand. "Mattie Holiday. Leader of myself, known associate of this army."

"Pleased to make your acquaintance," said Rattlesnake. Her handshake was firm, her hand dry and warm.

She turned her formidable gaze on Sammy, who grinned broadly.

"Oh, I'm just along for the ride," he said. "Sammy Collins."

Raccoon held up her cell phone. "I'm going outside to try one more time for Bonobo before we go into the bunker and are incommunicado." She spun on her heel and headed outside.

Rattlesnake turned to Mattie. "Your sister has caused some stir inside."

"Tillie?" Giovani snapped to attention, jumping on her words before Mattie could say anything. "She got free?"

"Yes." Rattlesnake gave him a small smile. "She is moving about with a small band of others I don't know, and also one of our own, Coyote."

"Coyote is free already?" said Meerkat. "You might have mentioned him among our assets."

"I don't recall listing out our assets," said Rattlesnake, baring her teeth again.

"Shouldn't we join up with them?" said Mattie.

"I believe they are heading our way," said Rattlesnake with a shrug. "But I have been rather too busy to keep my eyes on them. Last I scried, they were on their way."

"You're able to use magic?" said Mattie. "I tried to turn on my seer sight, but it didn't work." She tried again, with the same result.

Rattlesnake shrugged, a sinuous movement. "You are not a Special."

Just then, Raccoon returned. "She's on her way. She'll join us in the Pontiff's quarters, but requests that we begin without her."

"Fine," said Chameleon. "Let's go."

***

"We're nearly there," said Coyote. He pointed toward a door at the end of the corridor they had just turned into. "That is the antechamber to the antechamber. Kind of like an airlock."

"We did come this way before," Sister Margaret reminded him.

"Right," said Coyote. "There will undoubtedly be extra guards, given the situation. Draw your weapons and prepare for a fight."

Tillie turned on her seer sight and readied herself for battle. She was the only one who didn't have any kind of bladed weapons on her, preferring to use magery and hand-to-hand combat. Even Trevor had taken a short sword from one of the guards he'd killed.

As they proceeded cautiously down the hall, Coyote stopped abruptly about ten feet from the door. "Somebody else has been here already," he said.

Tillie extended her seer sight further to see what had happened. The room was full of orange-clad corpses. "The Harpers?" she guessed.

"They would have said something, I'm sure," said Amy.

"Let's take a closer look," said Coyote. He opened the door and the group filed in, crowding into the small room.

Tillie crouched beside a body, turning it over to examine its wounds. The man had been stabbed in the belly and had his throat slit.

"A two-handed fighter," said Sister Margaret. "Sword in one hand and a dagger in the other. This is the work of a professional."

"*A* professional?" said Nicole. "You think just one person did this?"

"Absolutely," she replied. She stood up and moved into the center of the room. "One person stood here in the center and fought them all. Look at the patterns."

Tillie looked, but could see no patterns. This was not her area of expertise.

"Rattlesnake," said Coyote with a grin. "Thank you, Rattlesnake."

Tillie glanced around the room, but he didn't seem to be speaking to anyone present.

"Listen, guys," said Coyote. "It's been real and all, but my people have clearly arrived, and I gotta go find them. You can find your own way out, right?" He nodded toward the open door, through which Tillie could see straight through to the outside world.

She hadn't been outside in over a week, and the breeze and the sunshine called to her.

"Thank you for your help," said Sister Margaret. "I'm sure we'll meet again before all of this is over."

"Wait," said Trevor. "Shouldn't we stay and fight?" He turned to Coyote. "You and your crew are going to go find and kill the Pontiff, aren't you?"

He nodded. "Don't take this the wrong way, but we've got it covered. You don't have anything we need." He eyed Sister Margaret. "Except maybe you. You're pretty bad-ass for a nun."

Sister Margaret grinned. "You haven't met a lot of other nuns, have you?"

"That's true," he admitted.

"I have to find my crew too," said Sister Margaret. "The army will be arriving any day, I'm sure."

"Really?" said Nicole. "How long have we been in there?"

"Only a couple of days," said Amy. "I thought they were a week out."

"They have their ways," said Sister Margaret. "Let's go."

"Thank you for all you've done for us," said Trevor, extending a hand to Coyote.

Coyote pulled Trevor in for a hug. "You'll always have an ally in me, friend."

Tillie was surprised to feel a small pang of jealousy. It's not like Trevor had never had friends other than her, but she felt like Coyote and Trevor had made a connection that was . . . different.

If Tillie was being honest with herself, something she'd always prided herself on, she and Trevor would probably never be as close again as they'd been before. And the sooner she owned up to that, the more likely she'd be able to salvage their friendship and allow it to evolve into something new.

And part of that was letting him go and do his own thing. She'd always felt like he put her and her needs before his own. It was time for that to end.

***

Mattie couldn't help but feel like she, Giovani, and Sammy were a bit superfluous as the Specials stalked down the halls of the bunker, the three ordinary mages trailing behind. Maybe it was ridiculous for them to even be there.

The Specials clearly didn't need them. They couldn't even do magery here in the bunker, while the Specials could. They didn't have the same fighting prowess either.

Rattlesnake had taken care of that entire room full of guards? Granted, the guards were a joke, but still – by pure numbers, they should have been able to overwhelm her, but she didn't even have a scratch on her.

Mattie wasn't sure even Sister Margaret would have come out of that fight without so much as breaking a nail.

The Specials marched around a bend ahead of them, and Mattie started to hasten her pace to keep up.

Then she became aware of a rhythmic sound behind her, and spun around.

Giovani and Sammy turned as well, swords out.

Mattie drew her own weapon. It sounded like someone running toward them, and they were gaining quickly.

A young man rounded the corner and slid to a halt right in front of them.

"Mattie!" he said. "How you doing? Long time, no see. Tillie and Trevor say hey."

"Jorge?" she said. "Or, I mean, it's Coyote, right?"

"Sure is."

"This is Coyote?" said Sammy. "Are any of you all not ridiculously handsome?"

Coyote grinned. "Can't think of anyone."

"Maybe I should be joining the Auditors instead of fighting them," said Sammy.

"Oh, it's far too late for that," said Coyote. "They're coming down. Nothing you could do to stop it. Everyone's always hooking up after a battle, though. Might get lucky soon."

"Oh, good tip," said Sammy.

"Speaking of battles," said Coyote. "You know where I can find some other Specials?"

"They went that way," said Mattie. She turned and led the way, trotting down the hall to catch up with the others. Sammy, Giovani, and Coyote followed.

They turned the corner, but the Specials must have gotten further ahead than she'd realized. Mattie sped up, moving into a full-on run, but at the end of this hallway, there was a fork. "Fuck," she said. "I don't know where they are."

"Where were they headed?" asked Coyote.

"The Pontiff," said Mattie.

"This way." Coyote took the lead, Mattie and her friends pounding after him.

Suddenly, the ground shook and there was a huge BOOM coming from off in the distance.

"That's coming from the front door," said Coyote. "Somebody's breaking into the bunker." His eyes went white and he pulled a marble out of his pocket, peering into it like a scrying stone. "They're taking a bulldozer to the hillside."

"The army," said Mattie. "They're here even faster than we thought."

"This ends today," said Coyote, his voice grim. "The Pontiff won't be killed by an army. He needs to be trapped and taken out in his den. If their machines open up the whole bunker, he will be able to escape."

"Can't he stitch out anyway?" asked Mattie.

"Nobody can stitch out of the Pontiff's chambers. Nobody can use any magery there, not even him. It's the most secure place in the bunker, and that's where he'll be. Come on." He began to run again, even as the earth continued to shake and pieces of walls and ceiling began to rain down on them.

***

Tillie watched as Father Sean smashed the wrecking ball into the hillside again and again. Finally, a blonde Harper watching from a cherry-picker above the site waved a flag at him, and he stopped.

As Father Sean reversed his machine, nuns and priests in bulldozers drove forward through the hole, smashing through walls and widening the opening. The three bulldozers disappeared into the bunker in a single file line down the broad hallway, presumably wreaking more damage as they went.

Tillie turned to glance over her shoulder, seeing rank after rank, hundreds of mages lined up, ready to rush into the bunker as soon as the signal was given. She wasn't sure there were nearly this many people still alive inside the place.

She wasn't sure they would all fit inside the bunker.

"This may have been a little bit of overkill," she murmured to Trevor, who stood beside her.

"Better overkill than underkill," said Sister Margaret. "But you're not wrong. We may do better by sending in small groups at a time."

Sister Margaret jogged over to Father Sean, who was still seated in his demolition machine, speaking into a walkie-talkie. He seemed to be in charge of the entire operation.

Tillie worried about Mattie and Giovani. That Harper man had said that they had gone in with a bunch of Special agents, people like Chameleon and Coyote; gone in to confront the Pontiff at the center of the bunker.

She had recognized two of the bulldozer operators from the convent. Those two would know Mattie and Giovani. Would the other? Or would they think they were agents? Mattie in particular was dressed the same as most of the Auditor agents.

Then again, she was also dressed the same as most of the Warrior Mage nuns who were here. And Giovani's suit, while beige instead of black, wasn't too dissimilar to the Harpers' suits.

Maybe they'd be okay.

"We need to get in there," said Trevor, echoing her thoughts. "We need to find our friends before those bulldozers do."

Sister Margaret trotted back toward them, and Tillie waved her over. "Can we be in the first wave?" she asked.

"Sure," said Sister Margaret. "Our whole gang can just turn right around and go right back in." She grinned at Amy and Nicole. "You game?"

Nicole gave her a bloodthirsty grin. "Let's go."

Amy just nodded and drew her sword, her eyes on the gaping hole that used to be an incredibly secure door.

Sister Margaret selected five more from the army gathered, all women, probably nuns. Tillie recognized a couple of them – that was Sister Regina, the seer Ida had always clashed with, and Sister Helen, who was in charge of security. Did that mean the entire convent was emptied out and no security was needed?

Tillie pushed that thought aside as irrelevant. Right now, she was mid-battle, and she needed to focus on finding Mattie and Giovani.

18.

Mattie slid to a halt outside a hole in the wall and followed Coyote through it. She stopped short just inside the room, her eyes widening at the pure, insane opulence of it.

Even through her boots, she could feel herself sinking into the forest green carpet. The deep green color of the floor was echoed in the green panels on the eight walls, which shone like gemstones. She wasn't entirely certain they weren't gems, in fact. Jade, maybe?

Inlaid into the panels were gold depictions of mage sigils. She recognized the symbols for the three mage disciplines, the hourglasses topped with lips for spellers, an eye for seers, and a hand mid-gesture for stitchers. Another panel had the Auditor symbol with the scales. She had never seen the other four.

As she gawked, Giovani gently pushed her forward, stepping through the hole in the wall behind her.

Mattie took another step into the room, making way for him and for Sammy behind him.

"Holy shit," said Sammy. He let out a low whistle as he took in the walls, the gigantic chandelier, the luxurious furniture.

"Yes, it's very impressive," said Coyote. "Where the fuck is everyone?"

"I don't see any doors," said Giovani. "I thought you said nobody could stitch in here; how do they get in and out generally?"

"Yeah, I can't imagine that smashing a hole in the wall is the standard method of entry," said Mattie.

"There!" said Sammy. He pointed to one of the corners, where the two walls didn't join exactly perfectly. "That's gotta be a door."

Coyote hurried forward and grasped the edge of the jade panel, using it to pry the entire section of wall back.

Mattie slipped through it after him and found herself in another preposterously sumptuous room, this one an echo of the ritual room

187

in Tillie's condo. Mattie remembered thinking that Tillie's ritual room was lavishly appointed, but this one blew hers out of the water.

But it was also empty of people. This room was rectangular and did have an ordinary door in the opposite wall.

Following Coyote, Mattie weaved her way between white leather couches on gold frames and past a white marble altar.

As soon as Coyote flung open the door, the sounds of battle rushed toward them. That was some impressive sound-proofing, if there were no mage shields involved.

***

As Sister Margaret led the way toward the bunker, a small, pale woman with silver hair appeared in front of them.

Tillie gasped as she almost ran into the woman, face to face.

"Hello," the woman said, her voice cold and expressionless. "You are Tillie Holiday."

"Yes, I know," said Tillie. "I have been for some time."

"I am Bonobo. I must join my brethren. I have heard of you. You may be useful."

"With a name like Bonobo, you've got to be a Special agent," said Trevor.

"Trevor Harper," said Bonobo. "You may come too."

"We're all coming," said Sister Margaret. Then she paused. "Wait, your last name is Harper? Like them?" She waved her hand toward where the black-suit-clad mages awaited their turn for action.

He stared at her. "Is that important right now? It's a common name, and yeah, it's been a little weird feeling like I'm at a family reunion or something, but—"

Sister Margaret waved him silent. "You're right. Not important." She turned back to Bonobo. "We're all coming," she repeated, crossing her arms and glaring at Bonobo, apparently not the slightest bit fazed by the woman's deadpan manner.

"All right." Bonobo extended her arms out in front of her, palms up.

Tillie placed a hand on the woman's upper arm, and Trevor put his right next to hers. Sister Margaret grabbed Bonobo's wrist and nodded to the other nuns, who all followed suit, arraying themselves along the Special's arms like they were hanging onto the handrail on a bus.

Bonobo moved her fingers and stitched them all into a hallway in the bunker. A few feet down the hall was a hole in the wall, just large enough for a person to step through.

"Are we outside my old cell?" asked Tillie with a frown.

"No," said Bonobo. "We are outside the Pontiff's quarters. You will not be able to use magery inside."

"Some of us have tattoos," said Trevor. "Special tattoos, I mean."

"Do you?" said Bonobo. "It won't help. I will not be able to use magery either. Nobody can. Not even *him*."

Him was the first word Bonobo had said that held any emotion, and it was pure, undiluted hatred.

"Come," said Bonobo. She stepped through the hole.

Tillie looked at Trevor, who shrugged and ducked to step through himself.

"Why the fuck did we bother with these tattoos?" Sister Margaret muttered, following Trevor.

"At least we'll be on even ground with everyone else," said Sister Helen.

Tillie shook her head. "I don't think anyone is on even ground with the Special agents." She stepped through the hole in the drywall. "Son of a bitch," she breathed as she looked around the room. "This is the tackiest thing I have ever seen."

"Yes," said Bonobo. "Is everyone here?"

Tillie glanced behind her and moved out of the way for the last of the nuns to enter. "Yeah, this is all of us."

Bonobo nodded and proceeded through the open door across the room.

Tillie followed into a ritual room that made hers look like a hovel. Through the open door at the other end, she could hear sounds of fighting.

***

Mattie paused to survey the fight. There were no guards here, clad in impractical orange bikini armor. These were clearly the elite, the Special agents. She recognized the same energy in the strangers as the Specials she'd met, a manner that held them apart from most, but connected them together, that said *I am pure warrior.*

Even at her most vulnerable, Chameleon had that aura. And she was not at that most vulnerable here. Here, she was in her element as she grappled with a wiry man with long brown hair pulled into a ponytail.

She wasn't sure what exactly told her, but Mattie was willing to bet that he was Weasel.

Rattlesnake was fighting with a dagger and short sword against a grinning maniac with a machete. You wouldn't think a machete could be wielded so skillfully in combat, but this person managed it. Their grin screamed Hyena.

Wolf was deep in heated conversation with a woman who was probably Hawk. The pair of them looked like they couldn't decide if they were about to strangle each other or start making out.

Meerkat fenced, his rapier flashing faster than she could track, against a large blonde woman, who moved with a somewhat clumsy-looking gait, but still managed to avoid Meerkat's sword time and again.

Mattie looked for Raccoon and Elephant, but didn't see them. She also didn't see the Pontiff, who she remembered from the battle in St. Louis as a cold-eyed old man who hid behind his guards.

A tapestry on the far side of the room flapped as though a breeze had hit it. There must be something behind it. Mattie jerked her head to Giovani and Sammy and began to make her way around the room, hugging the wall to avoid the fighting.

She staggered as Chameleon threw her opponent against the wall right in front of her. Drawing her sword, Mattie thrust it toward the man's belly.

He twisted out of the way, but Chameleon kicked him forward, and Mattie found herself staring into his eyes as she skewered him and the light slowly died in them.

"Ugh!" Reflexively, Mattie dropped the sword, her breath shaky. She'd killed in battle before, but never so intimately. Catching her breath again, she reached forward and pulled her sword out of Weasel's body, wiping it clean on another tapestry that hung beside her.

Chameleon had already moved on, drawing a knife and throwing herself into Meerkat's battle against the heavyweight.

Looking around, Mattie saw that Coyote was fighting alongside Rattlesnake.

Someone touched Mattie's arm and she whirled to find Giovani, gesturing toward the hidden door. "Right," she murmured. She followed him around the room.

As they reached their destination, a blood chilling shriek sounded from the entrance, and Mattie spun around again to see a small elderly woman flinging herself into the fray, attacking Wolf and his debate partner.

"Let me guess," said Sammy. "Bonobo."

"Probably," said Mattie. She followed Giovani into the next room.

***

Tillie entered the bedroom just in time to see Giovani disappear behind a tapestry across the room, followed by Mattie and Sammy. "What the hell is Sammy doing here?" she asked Trevor. "He's going to get himself killed."

"Any of us could get killed at any moment," said Sister Regina. "It's war. Sammy has raw power and good instincts."

"We'd better go after him, nevertheless," said Tillie. She grasped Trevor's hand and the pair of them began hurrying along the wall.

"Which of these people are on our side?" said Sister Helen, behind her.

"We'll take our cues from Chameleon and Bonobo," said Sister Margaret.

Tillie glanced back just before she ducked behind the tapestry, and saw Sister Margaret dispatch the heavy woman Chameleon had been fighting.

Then she stepped through the doorway into another, smaller workroom, this one starkly bare in contrast to the rooms she had just passed through – a concrete square similar to the cell she'd been kept in, but with a small table, a scrying stone, and a chair.

These had been pushed aside, and a familiar elderly man dressed in a priest-like robe sat in the chair, a small, cruel smile playing across his lips.

The Pontiff's cold eyes met Tillie's and his smile grew. This had to be the real Pontiff – if no magery was possible in this room, there was no possibility of an illusion spell.

She began to edge around the wall again, ignoring the fight going on in the middle of the room.

The room was too small to get around it, however, so she turned her attention back to see that Trevor was hovering as though unsure how to jump in.

Mattie, Giovani, and Sammy seemed to be fighting by the side of a tiny woman and a slim buzz-haired person of indeterminate gender. Their opponents, though only two, were fighting hard and consisted of a tall, fierce-looking woman with deep brown skin and a longsword, and a small, insanely quick man who fought with two hatchets.

***

As Mattie dodged one hatchet and ducked to avoid the other, she spun and saw the Pontiff reach forward, a wide smile on his face, and punch a button on the table in front of him.

With a crashing sound, a clear wall fell from the ceiling, landing in front of her, separating her from the creepy cult leader.

Mattie pivoted and saw that they were surrounded on all four sides and above by the plexiglass cage.

The woman who had been fighting Elephant had escaped, but the man with the hatchets was trapped inside with them.

The fighting inside the cage paused as Mattie, Giovani, and Sammy looked around in confusion. Elephant and Raccoon looked grim.

Raccoon stepped forward and grabbed Hatchet-Man by the collar. His weapons fell to the floor. "What is this?" she hissed.

He smirked, but didn't respond.

"Whatever it is, you will share our fate," Elephant pointed out.

Before he could say anything, an odorous vapor began to flood the cage.

"Poison!" Mattie shouted. She dimly saw that the fight outside the cage was raging on and it appeared that more people had filled the room, but she couldn't wait for anyone to free them. The Pontiff didn't strike her as someone who would put something innocuous in their air. It was almost certainly fatal.

Raccoon and Elephant began to frantically move their fingers, trying to stitch themselves out of the cage, but of course no magery could be used in the Pontiff's quarters.

Holding her breath as best she could, Mattie grabbed one of the fallen hatchets, elbowing Sammy out of the way and lifting the weapon over her head, smashing it down into the wall in front of her, over and over again.

Giovani followed suit with the other ax, pounding the opposite wall.

Finally, the wall in front of Mattie began to crack. She gasped for air and shifted her hands, gripping the top and bottom of the handle and swinging it like a battering ram into the vulnerable spot.

Beside her, Sammy began to punch at the wall, and for a few strokes, they fell into a rhythm – hatchet, fist, hatchet, fist, until finally, Sammy's bloody fist crashed through, and the wall shattered to sharp pieces.

Sammy stumbled forward, only to meet the tall woman with her longsword.

Mattie rushed into the fray, raising the hatchet and deflecting the sword away from Sammy's neck. It bit into his arm, and he howled in pain.

***

As Tillie whirled to meet another opponent, time seemed to slow down. She coughed and stumbled slightly as the air thickened with the poison from the broken box in the middle of the room.

Giovani, newly freed from the cage, slashed at the woman's wrist, his blade cutting into it deeply, and she dropped her dagger with a bellow.

Tillie regained her footing and punched her opponent in the side of the head, so she crumpled to the floor.

Looking around, she saw Mattie slash with her hatchet at a tall woman in front of her. Time slowed further, and Tillie watched as Mattie's foe fell.

The air grew clearer again as the poison dispersed in the larger space.

Pivoting, Mattie pulled a dagger out of a sheath on her upper arm and threw it toward the Pontiff. It stuck in the man's shoulder, and his frigid smile turned to a grimace.

The man whose hatchets Mattie had taken screamed and rushed at Mattie, who dodged and took two steps closer to the Pontiff, swinging her ax in a wide arc.

A head hit the floor.

Then the hatchet man screamed again and he picked up a longsword from the floor. It swished through the air.

Something flew across the room and a spray of blood smacked against Tillie's face.

She watched in horror as an armor-clad body swayed, headless, and Trevor reflexively caught something in his arms, lurching backward.

Tillie fell to her knees beside her fallen sister as Trevor cried out and dropped Mattie's head beside her. As her knees hit the floor, time returned to its normal speed.

The room was suddenly packed full of far too many people.

Numbly, Tillie reached out a hand to touch Mattie's limp arm. She grabbed her hand, half expecting Mattie to squeeze back, but there was no reaction.

Out of the corner of her eye, she saw the other head that had fallen, its eyes still cold, that cold grimace still plastered across it, and something inside of her knew that they had won.

The Pontiff was dead.

But so was Mattie.

Tillie remained, frozen on her knees as battle continued around her. She was vaguely aware of screams of pain, clashes of weapons, the rising smell of blood and sweat and the other horrors of a battle.

Finally, the sounds quieted, and the battle was over. Trevor grabbed her arms and hauled her bodily up, wrapping her in his arms as he sobbed.

"Mattie," mumbled Tillie. "Is she really . . . ?"

"Yes," said Trevor, his voice broken. "She's really gone."

"Oh." She couldn't think of anything else to say, too shocked even to cry. An absurd thought pushed its way into her mind. "She killed the Pontiff, though, didn't she?"

"Yes," said Trevor. His arms tightened around her.

Suddenly, convulsively, she pushed him away. "You don't have to put me first anymore," she said. "That's not fair to you."

"Okay," he said, quietly. "I won't."

"Good." She looked around the room. Giovani was nowhere to be seen, and most of the Specials – except the ones who were dead and lying on the floor – were gone as well.

Sister Abigail, the doctor from the convent, was working with another nun, putting Sammy onto a stretcher. "What happened to Sammy?" she asked. "Is he okay?"

Trevor shook his head. "I don't know." His breath caught. "I hope so. We should leave. We're not wounded and– We should leave."

Tillie nodded. She watched more nuns come in, saw them begin to gather up the dead, stacking the bodies on a stainless steel rolling cart. She had to leave – couldn't watch someone impassively deal with Mattie in that same way.

Tillie also knew, in some logical corner of her mind, that her emotions would catch up, and she knew she didn't want to be here when they did.

Wrapping an arm around Trevor, not sure if it was to support him or for him to support her, she began to walk slowly out of the Pontiff's quarters and then out of the bunker into the sunshine.

19.

Tillie opened the door to her condo and walked inside. She waited for Giovani to walk past her and then closed it behind him.

She sat down on the green chaise lounge, the chaise lounge that had been her mother's favorite, the one Mom had spent most of the last year of her life on, as cancer ravaged her body, before she'd been admitted to the hospital to die.

Mattie had been the one holding their mother's hand when she'd passed away, and it had taken a toll on her psyche.

Tillie had always known that, but she hadn't realized exactly how hard it could hit you, to hold a loved one's hand as they died.

Of course, Mattie had already been dead when Tillie had grabbed her hand.

That didn't make it any easier.

"I guess I should go get my cat from Scott," said Tillie, her voice dull. "Do you want to wait here or come with me?"

"Are you sure you wouldn't rather be alone?" asked Giovani. He sat down beside her and brushed a lock of hair away from her face, then dropped his hand quickly, as though he hadn't meant to do that. "I can go and stay with Trevor for a while or get a room at the convent."

"No!" Tillie, turning toward him quickly. "No, I need someone."

"Wouldn't you rather have Trevor here?" he asked. "Maybe the two of you should mourn together."

She shook her head. Her hair fell back in front of her face. She'd been growing it out so that she and Mattie would look more similar and would be better able to pull off the illusion that they were one person.

"I guess I'm Mattie now," she said. "Officially. I mean, she's actually dead, and I'm officially dead, so I guess I have to really be her."

"Do you feel like her?" asked Giovani.

"I barely feel like me," said Tillie. "But I don't feel like Mattie either."

"You're the only Mathilda Holiday now," said Giovani, softly. "I've gone through some identity changes myself. Taking on a new name can be . . . cleansing."

"Mathilda," said Tillie. "Mattie and I both always hated being called that." She laughed, and it sounded strange. She hadn't laughed since. . . .

Well, she hadn't laughed in the week since the battle. She hadn't cried either.

"Do you feel more like a Mathilda than a Mattie or a Tillie?" said Giovani.

"Yeah," said Mathilda. "I do." She smiled and it felt genuine, even as tears began to fall at last.

Epilogue

Trevor stood and shook the interviewer's hand across his desk. "I'm excited about this opportunity, and look forward to hearing from you soon," he said.

"You know what?" said Cardinal Neubacher, releasing his hand. "I don't think you need to wait. We're in dire need of more Warrior Mage Librarians with everything that's been going on, and you're just the kind of mage we're looking for."

"Really?" said Trevor. "That's fantastic to hear."

"And I think I have just the partner for you," Cardinal Neubacher continued. "She's on site, if you'd like to meet with her."

"That would be great," said Trevor.

"I think you two will balance each other out really nicely." The Cardinal walked around his desk and opened the door. "If you'd like to follow me."

Trevor walked behind him out into the hallway.

It had been a little over a month since the Battle of Broken Bunker, as it was being called in mage circles. He'd returned to St. Louis to find that he'd missed too many days of work and his job had replaced him. He didn't fight too hard for it – somehow, after all of that, he couldn't stomach the mundanity of going back to working a register at a grocery store.

He needed something bigger.

And he hated to admit it, even to himself, but he needed space from Tillie – Mathilda as she was calling herself these days – and she needed space from him. They would always be close friends, but she needed to figure herself out, and Giovani was the person to help her do that, not him.

Giovani was still living in Mathilda's condo, but he'd moved into her bedroom, and Trevor was glad. They were perfect together, and there was no room for Trevor to be what he had been to her in what he now thought of as the before-times.

So he'd begun looking for jobs that involved magery and would take him out of St. Louis. He'd quickly realized that meant working for the Vatican.

Cardinal Neubacher paused, bringing Trevor back to the present. "This is her office," he said. "I'll go ahead and leave you here. Will you be able to find your own way out, when you've finished chatting?"

"Absolutely," said Trevor. "Thank you so much."

"Not at all," said Cardinal Neubacher. "I will see you back here on Monday to process your paperwork, and I'm sure we'll have an assignment for the two of you within a week or so."

"Great." Trevor watched the Cardinal bustle back down the hall, and knocked on the door.

"Come in," said a familiar, slightly accented voice from within.

Trevor threw back his head and laughed. He opened the door.

"Well, look what the cat dragged in," said Sister Margaret with a broad grin, swinging her feet up onto her desk. "How the fuck are you?"

***

This concludes the Mathilda Holiday series. Thank you for reading! Trevor and Sister Margaret's story will continue in the upcoming *Warrior Mage Librarians* series, and I imagine there will be cameo appearances from other characters, including the remaining Mathilda, Giovani, Sammy, Coyote, and Chameleon.

Remember all through the last few books, when there were hints of Things Happening from the Sisters of Saint Joan and other Catholic types? Well, you'll find out more about those things in the next series. Expect it on Kickstarter in June 2023 and on retailers starting in Fall 2023.

About the Author

Anna McCluskey is an independent fantasy author known for her witty dialogue, whimsical storylines, and immersive style. Anna lives in rural Oregon with her husband and way too many pets and plants.

Read more at https://annamccluskey.com.

www.ingramcontent.com/pod-product-compliance
Lightning Source LLC
Chambersburg PA
CBHW032116020726
47494CB00007BA/2106